FRENZIED
FICTION

Stephen Leacock

FRENZIED FICTION

Introduction: David Dooley

General Editor: Malcolm Ross

New Canadian Library No. 48

MCCLELLAND AND STEWART LIMITED

First published in 1919 by John Lane, the Bodley Head

© McClelland and Stewart Limited, 1965

Introduction © McClelland and Stewart Limited 1971

The Canadian Publishers
McClelland and Stewart Limited
25 Hollinger Road, Toronto

0-7710-9148-6

PRINTED AND BOUND IN CANADA
BY T. H. BEST PRINTING COMPANY LIMITED
DON MILLS, ONTARIO

❧ CONTENTS ❧

	INTRODUCTION	vii
I.	*My Revelations as a Spy*	15
II.	*Father Knickerbocker: A Fantasy*	24
III.	*The Prophet in Our Midst*	35
IV.	*Personal Adventures in the Spirit World*	40
V.	*The Sorrows of a Summer Guest*	49
VI.	*To Nature and Back Again*	59
VII.	*The Cave-Man as He Is*	68
VIII.	*Ideal Interviews—*	
	I. *With a European Prince*	75
	II. *With Our Greatest Actor*	79
	III. *With Our Greatest Scientist*	83
	IV. *With Our Typical Novelists*	88
IX.	*The New Education*	95

v

X.	*The Errors of Santa Claus*	101
XI.	*Lost in New York*	105
XII.	*This Strenuous Age*	109
XIII.	*The Old, Old Story of How Five Men Went Fishing*	113
XIV.	*Back from the Land*	120
XV.	*The Perplexity Column as Done by the Jaded Journalist*	128
XVI.	*Simple Stories of Success, or How to Succeed in Life*	131
XVII.	*In Dry Toronto*	138
XVIII.	*Merry Christmas*	148
	THE AUTHOR	157

WITH his first humorous book, *Literary Lapses* (1910), Leacock established a reputation and won a following; his biographer Ralph L. Curry tells us that for the next fifteen years he was the best-selling humorist in the English language. Each year brought his addicts one more alliteratively entitled volume: *Nonsense Novels* in 1911, *Sunshine Sketches of a Little Town* in 1912, *Behind the Beyond* in 1913, *Arcadian Adventures with the Idle Rich* in 1914, *Moonbeams from the Larger Lunacy* in 1915, and *Further Foolishness* in 1916 (plus other works in the latter two years). A gap came in 1917, however, when Leacock was kept busy lecturing on behalf of the Belgian relief fund. During his lecture tour, he eventually settled on one humorous address which he gave again and again under the title *Frenzied Fiction*; when he brought out a book in 1919, he used this title for it.

In its review of *Nonsense Novels* the *Spectator* said: "We can assure our readers who delight in mere joyous desipience that they will find a rich harvest of laughter in the purely irresponsible outpourings of Professor Leacock's fancy." "Desipience" means folly or trifling, and the comment suggests the view of Leacock which Robertson Davies has described and deprecated – as a funny fellow who loved all mankind and passed his life in an atmosphere of easy laughter, varied with plunges into economics. Curry shares this view at least partially; he writes that Leacock decided early "that all good humor must be without harm" and that "There was evident in all his humorous writing a kindness and lack of malice which was rare." But, as both Davies and George Whalley show, there are deep and dark currents in Leacock; in his introduction to *My Discovery of England*, Whalley shows that Leacock's imagination was often bizarre and sometimes even macabre. Something very different from sunny and tolerant humour can be found in Chapter 8 of *My Discovery*, where an American is envisioned as describing the advent of prohibition in England and concludes his letter with the remark that the upper classes need not fear that their pleasures will be curtailed: "In fact you will find that, just as in America, the benefit of prohibition is intended to fall on the poorer classes. There is no desire to interfere with the rich."

Frenzied Fiction is set against the dark background of the Great War, and the second item, in fact, deals with the American entry into the war in 1917. Curiously, it begins by conjuring up an image of degeneration: Washington Irving's homely old Father Knickerbocker has become a nattily dressed man-about-town, with a keen eye for blondes. The attack is fairly direct, except for one subtle barb inserted early: Leacock takes from an old account of New York a description of a pleasant promenade near the Battery where the citizens were accustomed to walk with their wives and repeats it with a variation – "the citizens walking with their wives, their own wives. . . ." The evidence of moral decline grows stronger and stronger until, when Knickerbocker jauntily offers him an introduction to the biggest swindler and the crookedest lawyer in the country, the narrator wonders whether the fine old spirit of New York is drowned in wine or suffocated in luxury. At the end, of course, luxury is cast off, and the spirit of patriotism and dedication with which the United States entered the War is strongly conveyed. The concluding piece in the volume is more melancholy; its title, "Merry Christmas", contains a sombre irony. Santa Claus appears here as a gaunt and broken figure who expects the floor to be mined and mistakes a pile of books for a machine gun; his expression is "as of one who has asked in vain the warmth and shelter of a human home. . . ."

Though the ending expresses the hope that war's sacrifices will not be vain in fairly conventional terms, before that Leacock has uttered a poignant lament for fatherless families and homeless children.

But the war did not subdue Leacock's sense of humour. He once said that writing was no trouble: "you just jot down ideas as they occur to you. The jotting is simplicity itself – it is the occurring which is difficult." So productive a humorist was bound to force the note occasionally; and even when he had a genuine comic inspiration it might sometimes be worked out in a contrived and mechanical way. But it is remarkable how often the "occurring" seemed to take place. In "My Revelations as a Spy", the burlesque quality is established in the very first paragraph, when the speaker tells of the shudder of apprehension which occurs "Whenever I enter a hotel and register myself as a Spy. . . ." The mockery of spy stories continues with excellent nonsensical details – the story of spies who recognize each other by movements of the eyelid so imperceptible that they cannot be seen, the mention of a footing so delicate that one single *faux pas* might prove to be a false step, and so on. Perhaps Leacock does not know what to do with his spy at the end, and goes too far when he makes him think of opening up a fruit store or a peanut stand, but before that he has constructed a number of very amusing situations, especially that of the spy unable to influence the American cabinet because no one in the American cabinet ever invites him out to dinner.

"The Prophet in our Midst" offers some excellent satire of the know-it-all who discourses on the Cypriotic suzerainty of the Porte, involves ententes with embroglios, and leaves his audience of plain men, who only wanted plain answers about what was happening in the war, hovering perilously between Zollvereins and Ausgleichs. But probably the best of the war pieces is "Back from the Land," with its legion of bankers, brokers, and engineers who go out to dig for victory – 50,000 warm hearts beating behind 50,000 pairs of oversize trousers held up by 50,000 polka-dot neckties. Here the level of comic fantasy is sustained throughout; it produces such gems as the paragraph on when to begin gardening, which always turns out to be the year before last, or earlier.

Leacock's method in this book is very often that of reducing things to absurdity. Modern trends in education lead, in his view, to girls taking field trips with Professors of Ambulation, and youths who protest that they are not loafing but earning credits in Introspection. Spiritualism, the vanity of actors, and the back-to-nature movement are treated in much the same way; the New England woods, for example, turn out to be far too heavily populated with men in union suits gnawing at the barks of trees. Similarly realism in fiction is taken to the point where the novelist says that if only he sits in his pig sty long enough his characters always come to him, and naturalism turns out to be the approach taken by the author of "Leaves from the Life of a Steam Laundry-woman," who is now planning to immerse herself in the pickle industry. Thus Leacock shows himself a master of one of the oldest and best of comic and satiric devices.

When Curry wrote that Leacock "represented in a way the paradox which is Canada. Born in England, he moved to Canada and wrote American humor," he stirred up a hornet's nest. The reviewers were quick to point out that the Canadian background was very important in Leacock's writings, and that, as J.B. Priestley had said, the best of Leacock's humour is quite different in outlook, manner, and style from British and American humour and expresses an essential Canadian quality. Perhaps the very mixture of British and American elements was characteristically Canadian. Leacock once made fun of a reviewer who thought he had found his recipe: "What is there, after all, in Professor Leacock's humour but a rather ingenious mixture of hyperbole and myosis?" "I am willing to admit," responded Leacock, "that it has been my custom in preparing an article of a humorous nature, to go down to the cellar and mix up half a gallon of myosis with a pint of hyperbole." Nevertheless the two terms do indicate two traditions of humour, an English tradition of understatement and an American tradition of exaggeration, traditions which Leacock himself analysed and discussed. When he said that American humour depended on making impossibility seem true, he revealed something about his own way of writing; the fantasy, the inventiveness, the exuberant flow of imagination seem very close to the American tradition. The opening of Mark Twain's burlesque of a 4th of

July Oration – "I was sired by the Great American Eagle and foaled by a continental dam" – is nonsense very much in Leacock's humorous vein. But the American tradition is often characterized by an almost uncontrollable fantasy, which produces the "tall story"; Davy Crockett, for example, could travel so fast that he had been known to strike fire against the wind, and he once escaped up Niagara Falls on an alligator. If, on the other hand, we read "My Revelations as a Spy", we find that the humour depends just as much on controlled or understated effects as it does on exaggeration.

But when Leacock writes in *My Discovery of England* that girls in girls' colleges speak their minds freely, whereas a girl in a place like McGill "sits for four years as silent as a frog full of shot," we hear an echo of Mark Twain's story of the celebrated jumping frog. A similarity to Twain in approach and method is suggested by a comparison which Leacock made between Twain and Dickens, in which he declared that the former is absolutely distinguished from the latter by the "humor of discomfiture written in the first person." As *Three Men in a Boat* and *The Diary of a Nobody* will show, this type of humour is not exclusively American; but Leacock cites and presumably followed an American precedent for it. Sometimes the "I" in a Leacock story deserves to be discomfited; the spy and the advocate of a return to nature are examples. Usually, however, he is sympathetic. He is sometimes the little man bewildered by the complexity of the modern world, though the early story "My Financial Career" is a more effective treatment of this theme than the soliloquy of the person lost in New York which we have in this volume. Again and again, however, we are invited to identify ourselves with a simple person who is harassed by some kind of complexity, obscurity, or pretentiousness. In "The Prophet in Our Midst," his silence offers a derisive commentary upon the self-styled expert in international affairs. In "This Strenuous Age," he is the sort of person who says with disgust, "I know quite a lot of men who have actually bought the new *Encyclopaedia Britannica*. What is more, they *read* the thing." In "Back from the Land", he ridicules such technical language as "a deep friable loam rich in nitrogen"; from the depth of his experience, he avers that "the only soils are earth, mud and dirt." This contrast between homespun naturalness and sophistication or pretentiousness of any kind is of course a familiar one in American humour.

One kind of pretentiousness against which the plain man rebels is the new puritanism. Leacock is no more worried about the war in this volume than he is about other threats to humane values, especially the campaign for prohibition. He can ridicule, in "How Five Men Went Fishing", the elaborate ritual which surrounds his favourite sport and which makes men think that what they want at five o'clock in the morning is a good "snort" or "snifter" of raw whisky. Yet he has a gloomy vision of people not only bathing in, but drinking, ice water. The speaker in "This Strenuous Age" is regretful and nostalgic:

. . I wish somehow that we could prohibit the use of alcohol and merely drink beer and whisky and gin as we used to. But these things, it appears, interfere with work. They have got to go.

The most telling attack on prohibition is "In Dry Toronto", which presents a Montrealer's view of Toronto in the days when it was still Toronto the Good and when it could be characterized by a Mr. Narrowpath. Mr. Narrowpath is friendly and helpful – "I've always a great liking for attending to other people's business" – and he is of course a canting hypocrite:

"Dreadful, isn't it?" said Mr. Narrowpath. "The sunken, depraved condition of your City of Montreal; actually *selling* whisky. Deplorable!" and with that he buried his face in the bubbles of the whisky and soda.

In *Frenzied Fiction*, Leacock woos American attention by using American narrators and American place names in some of his pieces, or else seeks universality by leaving the settings of some others unparticularized. Nevertheless, though he suggests somewhat apologetically that his African readers may want to read it under the title "In Dry Timbuctoo," "In Dry Toronto," one of the best things in the book, is entirely Canadian in atmosphere and feeling:

xii

I pulled up the blind and looked out of the window and there was the good old city, with the bright sun sparkling on its church spires and on the bay spread out at its feet. It looked quite unchanged : just the same pleasant old place, as cheerful, as self-conceited, as kindly, as hospitable, as quarrelsome, as wholesome, as moral and as loyal and as disagreeable as it always was.

D. J. DOOLEY

St. Michael's College,
University of Toronto

❧ I ❧

My
Revelations
as a Spy

IN MANY people the very name "Spy" excites a shudder of apprehension; we Spies, in fact, get quite used to being shuddered at. None of us Spies mind it at all. Whenever I enter a hotel and register myself as a Spy I am quite accustomed to see a thrill of fear run round the clerks, or clerk, behind the desk.

Us Spies or We Spies – for we call ourselves both – are thus a race apart. None know us. All fear us. Where do we live? Nowhere. Where are we? Everywhere. Frequently we don't know ourselves where we are. The secret orders that we receive come from so high up that it is often forbidden to us even to ask where we are. A friend of mine, or at least a Fellow Spy – us Spies have no friends – one of the most brilliant men in the Hungarian Secret Service, once spent a month in New York under the impression that he was in Winnipeg. If this happened to the most brilliant, think of the others.

All, I say, fear us. Because they know and have reason to know our power. Hence, in spite of the prejudice against us, we are able to move everywhere, to lodge in the best hotels, and enter any society that we wish to penetrate.

Let me relate an incident to illustrate this : a month ago I entered one of the largest of the New York hotels which I will merely call the B. hotel without naming it : to do so might blast it. We Spies, in fact, never *name* a hotel. At the most we indicate it by a number known only to ourselves, such as 1, 2, or 3.

On my presenting myself at the desk the clerk informed me that he had no room vacant. I knew this of course to be a mere subterfuge; whether or not he suspected that I was a Spy I cannot say. I was muffled up, to avoid recognition, in a long overcoat with the collar turned up and reaching well above my ears, while the black beard and the moustache, that I had slipped on in entering the hotel, concealed my face. "Let me speak a moment to the manager," I said. When he came I beckoned him aside and taking his ear in my hand I breathed two words into it. "Good heavens!" he gasped, while his face turned as pale as ashes. "Is it enough?" I asked. "Can I have a room, or must I breathe again?" "No, no," said the manager, still trembling. Then, turning to the clerk: "Give this gentleman a room," he said, "and give him a bath."

What these two words are that will get a room in New York at once I must not divulge. Even now, when the veil of secrecy is being lifted, the international interests involved are too complicated to permit it. Suffice it to say that if these two had failed I know a couple of others still better.

I narrate this incident, otherwise trivial, as indicating the astounding ramifications and the ubiquity of the international spy system. A similar illustration occurs to me as I write. I was walking the other day with another man, on upper B. way between the T. Building and the W. Garden. "Do you see that man over there?" I said, pointing from the side of the street on which we were walking on the sidewalk to the other side opposite to the side that we were on.

"The man with the straw hat?" he asked. "Yes, what of him?"

"Oh, nothing," I answered, "except that he's a Spy!"

"Great heavens!" exclaimed my acquaintance, leaning up against a lamp-post for support. "A Spy! How do you know that? What does it mean?"

I gave a quiet laugh — we Spies learn to laugh very quietly. "Ha!" I said, "that is *my* secret, my friend. *Verbum sapientius! Che sarà sarà! Yodel doodle doo!*"

My acquaintance fell in a dead faint upon the street. I

watched them take him away in an ambulance. Will the reader be surprised to learn that among the white-coated attendants who removed him I recognized no less a person than the famous Russian Spy, Poulispantzoff. What he was doing there I could not tell. No doubt his orders came from so high up that he himself did not know. I had seen him only twice before – once when we were both disguised as Zulus at Buluwayo, and once in the interior of China, at the time when Poulispantzoff made his secret entry into Thibet concealed in a tea-case. He was inside the tea-case when I saw him; so at least I was informed by the coolies who carried it. Yet I recognized him instantly. Neither he nor I, however, gave any sign of recognition other than an imperceptible movement of the outer eyelid. (We Spies learn to move the outer lid of the eye so imperceptibly that it cannot be seen.) Yet after meeting Poulispantzoff in this way I was not surprised to read in the evening papers a few hours afterward that the uncle of the young King of Siam had been assassinated. The connection between these two events I am unfortunately not at liberty to explain; the consequences to the Vatican would be too serious. I doubt if it could remain top-side up.

These, however, are but passing incidents in a life filled with danger and excitement. They would have remained unrecorded and unrevealed, like the rest of my revelations, were it not that certain recent events have to some extent removed the seal of secrecy from my lips. The death of a certain royal sovereign makes it possible for me to divulge things hitherto undivulgeable. Even now I can only tell a part, a small part, of the terrific things that I know. When more sovereigns die I can divulge more. I hope to keep on divulging at intervals for years. But I am compelled to be cautious. My relations with the Wilhelmstrasse, with Downing Street and the Quai d'Orsay, are so intimate, and my footing with the Yildiz Kiosk and the Waldorf-Astoria and Childs' Restaurants are so delicate, that a single *faux pas* might prove to be a false step.

It is now seventeen years since I entered the Secret Service of the G. empire. During this time my activities have taken me into every quarter of the globe, at times even into every eighth or sixteenth of it.

It was I who first brought back word to the Imperial Chancellor of the existence of an Entente between England and France. "Is there an Entente?" he asked me, trembling with excitement, on my arrival at the Wilhelmstrasse. "Your Excellency," I said, "there is." He groaned. "Can you stop it?" he asked. "Don't ask me," I said sadly. "Where must we strike?" demanded the Chancellor. "Fetch me a map," I said. They did so. I placed my finger on the map. "Quick, quick," said the Chancellor, "look where his finger is." They lifted it up. "Morocco!" they cried. I had meant it for Abyssinia but it was too late to change. That night the warship *Panther* sailed under sealed orders. The rest is history, or at least history and geography.

In the same way it was I who brought word to the Wilhelmstrasse of the *rapprochement* between England and Russia in Persia. "What did you find?" asked the Chancellor as I laid aside the Russian disguise in which I had travelled. "A *Rapprochement!*" I said. He groaned. "They seem to get all the best words," he said.

I shall always feel, to my regret, that I am personally responsible for the outbreak of the present war. It may have had ulterior causes. But there is no doubt that it was precipitated by the fact that, for the first time in seventeen years, I took a six weeks' vacation in June and July of 1914. The consequences of this careless step I ought to have foreseen. Yet I took such precautions as I could. "Do you think," I asked, "that you can preserve the *status quo* for six weeks, merely six weeks, if I stop spying and take a rest?" "We'll try," they answered. "Remember," I said, as I packed my things, "keep the Dardanelles closed; have the Sandjak of Novi Bazaar properly patrolled, and let the Dobrudja remain under a *modus vivendi* till I come back."

Two months later, while sitting sipping my coffee at a Kurhof in the Schwarzwald, I read in the newspapers that a German army had invaded France and was fighting the French, and that the English expeditionary force had crossed the Channel. "This," I said to myself, "means war." As usual, I was right.

It is needless for me to recount here the life of busy activity that falls to a Spy in wartime. It was necessary for me to be here, there and everywhere, visiting all the best hotels, watering-places, summer resorts, theatres, and places of amusement. It was necessary, moreover, to act with the utmost caution and to assume an air of careless indolence in order to lull suspicion asleep. With this end in view I made a practice of never rising till ten in the morning. I breakfasted with great leisure, and contented myself with passing the morning in a quiet stroll, taking care, however, to keep my ears open. After lunch I generally feigned a light sleep, keeping my ears shut. A table d'hôte dinner, followed by a visit to the theatre, brought the strenuous day to a close. Few Spies, I venture to say, worked harder than I did.

It was during the third year of the war that I received a peremptory summons from the head of the Imperial Secret Service at Berlin, Baron Fisch von Gestern. "I want to see you," it read. Nothing more. In the life of a Spy one learns to think quickly, and to think is to act. I gathered as soon as I received the despatch that for some reason or other Fisch von Gestern was anxious to see me, having, as I instantly inferred, something to say to me. This conjecture proved correct.

The Baron rose at my entrance with military correctness and shook hands.

"Are you willing," he inquired, "to undertake a mission to America?"

"I am," I answered.

"Very good. How soon can you start?"

"As soon as I have paid the few bills that I owe in Berlin," I replied.

"We can hardly wait for that," said my chief, "and in case it might excite comment. You must start to-night!"

"Very good," I said.

"Such," said the Baron, "are the Kaiser's orders. Here is an American passport and a photograph that will answer the purpose. The likeness is not great, but it is sufficient."

"But," I objected, abashed for a moment, "this photograph is of a man with whiskers and I am, unfortunately, cleanshaven."

"The orders are imperative," said Gestern, with official hauteur. "You must start to-night. You can grow whiskers this afternoon."

"Very good," I replied.

19

"And now to the business of your mission," continued the Baron. "The United States, as you have perhaps heard, is making war against Germany."

"I have heard so," I replied.

"Yes," continued Gestern. "The fact has leaked out – how, we do not know – and is being widely reported. His Imperial Majesty has decided to stop the war with the United States."

I bowed.

"He intends to send over a secret treaty of the same nature as the one recently made with his recent Highness the recent Czar of Russia. Under this treaty Germany proposes to give to the United States the whole of equatorial Africa and in return the United States is to give to Germany the whole of China. There are other provisions, but I need not trouble you with them. Your mission relates, not to the actual treaty, but to the preparation of the ground."

I bowed again.

"You are aware, I presume," continued the Baron, "that in all high international dealings, at least in Europe, the ground has to be prepared. A hundred threads must be unravelled. This the Imperial Government itself cannot stoop to do. The work must be done by agents like yourself. You understand all this already, no doubt?"

I indicated my assent.

"These, then, are your instructions," said the Baron, speaking slowly and distinctly, as if to impress his words upon my memory. "On your arrival in the United States you will follow the accredited methods that are known to be used by all the best Spies of the highest diplomacy. You have no doubt read some of the books, almost manuals of instruction, that they have written?"

"I have read many of them," I said.

"Very well. You will enter, that is to say, enter and move everywhere in the best society. Mark specially, please, that you must not only *enter* it but you must *move*. You must, if I may put it so, get a move on."

I bowed.

"You must mix freely with the members of the Cabinet. You must dine with them. This is a most necessary matter and one to be kept well in mind. Dine with them often in such a way as to make yourself familiar to them. Will you do this?"

"I will," I said.

"Very good. Remember also that in order to mask your purpose you must constantly be seen with the most fashionable and most beautiful women of the American capital. Can you do this?"

"Can I?" I said.

"You must if need be" – and the Baron gave a most significant look which was not lost upon me – "carry on an intrigue with one or, better, with several of them. Are you ready for it?"

"More than ready," I said.

"Very good. But this is only a part. You are expected also to familiarize yourself with the leaders of the great financial interests. You are to put yourself on such a footing with them as to borrow large sums of money from them. Do you object to this?"

"No," I said frankly, "I do not."

"Good! You will also mingle freely in Ambassadorial and foreign circles. It would be well for you to dine, at least once a week, with the British Ambassador. And now one final word" – here Gestern spoke with singular impressiveness – "as to the President of the United States."

"Yes," I said.

"You must mix with him on a footing of the most open-handed friendliness. Be at the White House continually. Make yourself in the fullest sense of the words the friend and adviser of the President. All this I think is clear. In fact, it is only what is done, as you know, by all the masters of international diplomacy."

"Precisely," I said.

"Very good. And then," continued the Baron, "as soon as you find yourself sufficiently *en rapport* with everybody, or I should say," he added in correction, for the Baron shares fully in the present German horror of imported French words, "when you find yourself sufficiently in enggeknüp-fterverwandtschaft with everybody, you may then proceed to advance your peace terms. And now, my dear fellow," said the Baron, with a touch of genuine cordiality, "one word more. Are you in need of money?"

21

"Yes," I said.

"I thought so. But you will find that you need it less and less as you go on. Meantime, good-bye, and best wishes for your mission."

Such was, such is, in fact, the mission with which I am accredited. I regard it as by far the most important mission with which I have been accredited by the Wilhelmstrasse. Yet I am compelled to admit that up to the present it has proved unsuccessful. My attempts to carry it out have been baffled. There is something perhaps in the atmosphere of this republic which obstructs the working of high diplomacy. For over five months now I have been waiting and willing to dine with the American Cabinet. They have not invited me. For four weeks I sat each night waiting in the J. hotel in Washington with my suit on ready to be asked. They did not come near me.

Nor have I yet received an invitation from the British Embassy inviting me to an informal lunch or to midnight supper with the Ambassador. Everybody who knows anything of the inside working of the international spy system will realize that without these invitations one can do nothing. Nor has the President of the United States given any sign. I have sent word to him, in cipher, that I am ready to dine with him on any day that may be convenient to both of us. He has made no move in the matter.

Under these circumstances an intrigue with any of the leaders of fashionable society has proved impossible. My attempts to approach them have been misunderstood – in fact, have led to my being invited to leave the J. hotel. The fact that I was compelled to leave it, owing to reasons that I cannot reveal, without paying my account, has occasioned unnecessary and dangerous comment. I connect it, in fact, with the singular attitude adopted by the B. hotel on my arrival in New York, to which I have already referred.

I have therefore been compelled to fall back on revelations and disclosures. Here again I find the American atmosphere singularly uncongenial. I have offered to reveal to the Secretary of State the entire family history of Ferdinand of Bulgaria for fifty dollars. He says it is not worth it. I have offered to the British Embassy the inside story of the Abdication of Constantine for five dollars. They say they know it,

22

and knew it before it happened. I have offered, for little more than a nominal sum, to blacken the character of every reigning family in Germany. I am told that it is not necessary.

Meantime, as it is impossible to return to Central Europe, I expect to open either a fruit store or a peanut stand very shortly in this great metropolis. I imagine that many of my former colleagues will soon be doing the same!

❧ II ❧

Father Knickerbocker:
A
Fantasy

IT HAPPENED quite recently – I think it must have been on April the second of 1917 – that I was making the long pilgrimage on a day-train from the remote place where I dwell to the city of New York. And as we drew near the city, and day darkened into night, I had fallen to reading from a quaint old copy of Washington Irving's immortal sketches of Father Knickerbocker and of the little town where once he dwelt.

I had picked up the book I know not where. Very old it apparently was and made in England. For there was pasted across the fly-leaf of it an extract from some ancient magazine or journal of a century ago, giving what was evidently a description of the New York of that day.

From reading the book I turned – my head still filled with the vision of Father Knickerbocker and Sleepy Hollow and Tarrytown – to examine the extract. I read it in a sort of half-doze, for the dark had fallen outside, and the drowsy throbbing of the running train attuned one's mind to dreaming of the past.

"The town of New York" – so ran the extract pasted in the little book – "is pleasantly situated at the lower extremity of the Island of Manhattan. Its recent progress has been so amazing that it is now reputed, on good authority, to harbour at least twenty thousand souls. Viewed from the sea, it presents, even at the distance of half a mile, a striking appearance owing to the number and beauty of its church spires, which rise high above the roofs and foliage and give to the place its characteristically religious aspect. The extreme end of the island is heavily fortified with cannon, commanding a range of a quarter of a mile, and forbidding all access to the harbour. Behind this Battery a neat greensward affords a pleasant promenade, where the citizens are accustomed to walk with their wives every morning after church."

"How I should like to have seen it!" I murmured to myself as I laid the book aside for a moment. "The Battery, the harbour and the citizens walking with their wives, their own wives, on the greensward."

Then I read on:

"From the town itself a wide thoroughfare, the Albany Post Road, runs meandering northward through the fields. It is known for some distance under the name of the Broad Way, and is so wide that four moving vehicles are said to be able to pass abreast. The Broad Way, especially in the springtime when it is redolent with the scent of clover and apple-blossoms, is a favourite evening promenade for the citizens – with their wives – after church. Here they may be seen any evening strolling toward the high ground overlooking the Hudson, their wives on one arm, a spyglass under the other, in order to view what they can see. Down the Broad Way may be seen moving also droves of young lambs with their shepherds, proceeding to the market, while here and there a goat stands quietly munching beside the road and gazing at the passers-by."

"It seems," I muttered to myself as I read, "in some ways but little changed after all."

"The town" – so the extract continued – "is not without its amusements. A commodious theatre presents with great success every Saturday night the plays of Shakespeare alternating with sacred concerts; the New Yorker, indeed, is celebrated throughout the provinces for his love of amusement and late hours. The theatres do not come out until long after nine o'clock, while for the gayer habitués two excellent restaurants serve fish, macaroni, prunes and other delicacies till long past ten at night. The dress of the New Yorker is correspondingly gay. In the other provinces the men wear nothing but plain suits of a rusty black, whereas in New York there are frequently seen suits of brown, snuff-colour and even of pepper-and-salt. The costumes of the New York women are equally daring, and differ notably from the quiet dress of New England.

"In fine, it is commonly said in the provinces that a New Yorker can be recognized anywhere, with his wife, by their modish costumes, their easy manners and their willingness to spend money – two, three and even five cents being paid for the smallest service."

"Dear me," I thought, as I paused a moment in my reading, "so they had begun it even then."

"The whole spirit of the place" – the account continued – "has recently been admirably embodied in literary form by an American writer, Mr. Washington Irving (not to be confounded with George Washington). His creation of Father Knickerbocker is so lifelike that it may be said to embody the very spirit of New York. The accompanying woodcut – which was drawn on wood especially for this periodical – recalls at once the delightful figure of Father Knickerbocker. The New Yorkers of to-day are accustomed, indeed, to laugh at Mr. Irving's fancy and to say that Knickerbocker belongs to a day long since past. Yet those who know tell us that the image of the amiable old gentleman, kindly but irascible, generous and yet frugal, loving his town and seeing little beyond it, may be held once and for all to typify the spirit of the place, without reference to any particular time or generation."

"Father Knickerbocker!" I murmured, as I felt myself dozing off to sleep, rocked by the motion of the car. "Father Knickerbocker, how strange if he could be here again and see the great city as we know it now! How different from his day! How I should love to go round New York and show it to him as it is."

So I mused and dozed till the very rumble of the wheels seemed to piece together in little snatches. "Father Knickerbocker – Father Knickerbocker – the Battery – the Battery – citizens walking with their wives, with their wives – their own wives" – until presently, I imagine, I must have fallen asleep altogether and knew no more till my journey was over and I found myself among the roar and bustle of the concourse of the Grand Central.

And there, lo and behold, waiting to meet me, was Father Knickerbocker himself! I know not how it happened, by what queer freak of hallucination or by what actual miracle – let those explain it who deal in such things – but there he stood before me, with an outstretched hand and a smile of greeting, Father Knickerbocker himself, the Embodied Spirit of New York.

"How strange," I said. "I was just reading about you in a book on the train and imagining how much I should like actually to meet you and to show you round New York."

The old man laughed in a jaunty way.

"Show *me* round?" he said. "Why, my dear boy, I *live* here."

"I know you did long ago," I said.

"I do still," said Father Knickerbocker. "I've never left the place. I'll show *you* around. But wait a bit – don't carry that handbag. I'll get a boy to call a porter to fetch a man to take it."

"Oh, I can carry it," I said. "It's a mere nothing."

"My dear fellow," said Father Knickerbocker, a little testily I thought, "I'm as democratic and as plain and simple as any man in this city. But when it comes to carrying a handbag in full sight of all this crowd, why, as I said to Peter Stuyvesant about – about" – here a misty look seemed to come over the old gentleman's face – "about two hundred years ago, I'll be hanged if I will. It can't be done. It's not up to date."

While he was saying this, Father Knickerbocker had beckoned to a group of porters.

"Take this gentleman's handbag," he said, "and you carry his newspapers, and you take his umbrella. Here's a quarter for you and a quarter for you and a quarter for you. One of you go in front and lead the way to a taxi."

"Don't you know the way yourself?" I asked in a half-whisper.

"Of course I do, but I generally like to walk with a boy in front of me. We all do. Only the cheap people nowadays find their own way."

Father Knickerbocker had taken my arm and was walking

27

along in a queer, excited fashion, senile and yet with a sort of forced youthfulness in his gait and manner.

"Now then," he said, "get into this taxi."

"Can't we *walk*?" I asked.

"Impossible," said the old gentleman. "It's five blocks to where we are going."

As we took our seats I looked again at my companion, this time more closely. Father Knickerbocker he certainly was, yet somehow strangely transformed from my pictured fancy of the Sleepy Hollow days. His antique coat with its wide skirt had, it seemed, assumed a modish cut as if in imitation of the bell-shaped spring overcoat of the young man about town. His three-cornered hat was set at a rakish angle till it looked almost like an up-to-date fedora. The great stick that he used to carry had somehow changed itself into the curved walking-stick of a Broadway lounger. The solid old shoes with their wide buckles were gone. In their place he wore narrow slippers of patent leather of which he seemed inordinately proud, for he had stuck his feet up ostentatiously on the seat opposite. His eyes followed my glance toward his shoes.

"For the fox-trot," he said. "The old ones were no good. Have a cigarette? These are Armenian, or would you prefer a Honolulan or a Nigerian? Now," he resumed, when we had lighted our cigarettes, "what would you like to do first? Dance the tango? Hear some Hawaiian music, drink cocktails, or what?"

"Why, what I should like most of all, Father Knickerbocker —"

But he interrupted me.

"There's a devilish fine woman! Look, the tall blonde one! Give me blondes every time!" Here he smacked his lips. "By gad, sir, the women in this town seem to get finer every century. What were you saying?"

"Why, Father Knickerbocker," I began, but he interrupted me again.

"My dear fellow," he said. "May I ask you not to call me *Father* Knickerbocker?"

"But I thought you were so old," I said humbly.

"Old! Me *old*! Oh, I don't know. Why, dash it, there are plenty of men as old as I am dancing the tango here every

28

night. Pray call me, if you don't mind, just Knickerbocker, or simply Knicky – most of the other boys call me Knicky. Now what's it to be?"

"Most of all," I said, "I should like to go to some quiet place and have a talk about the old days."

"Right," he said. "We're going to just the place now – nice quiet dinner, a good quiet orchestra, Hawaiian, but quiet, and lots of women." Here he smacked his lips again, and nudged me with his elbow. "Lots of women, bunches of them. Do you like women?"

"Why, Mr. Knickerbocker," I said hesitatingly, "I suppose – I —"

The old man sniggered as he poked me again in the ribs. "You bet you do, you dog!" he chuckled. "We *all* do. For me, I confess it, sir, I can't sit down to dinner without plenty of women, stacks of them, all round me."

Meantime the taxi had stopped. I was about to open the door and get out.

"Wait, wait," said Father Knickerbocker, his hand upon my arm, as he looked out of the window. "I'll see somebody in a minute who'll let us out for fifty cents. None of us here ever gets in or out of anything by ourselves. It's bad form. Ah, here he is!"

A moment later we had passed through the portals of a great restaurant, and found ourselves surrounded with all the colour and tumult of a New York dinner *à la mode*. A burst of wild music, pounded and thrummed out on ukuleles by a group of yellow men in Hawaiian costume, filled the room, helping to drown or perhaps only serving to accentuate the babel of talk and the clatter of dishes that arose on every side. Men in evening dress and women in all the colours of the rainbow, *décolleté* to a degree, were seated at little tables, blowing blue smoke into the air, and drinking green and yellow drinks from glasses with thin stems. A troupe of *cabaret* performers shouted and leaped on a little stage at the side of the room, unheeded by the crowd.

"Ha ha!" said Knickerbocker, as we drew in our chairs to a table. "Some place, eh? There's a peach! Look at her! Or do you like better that lazy-looking brunette next to her?"

Mr. Knickerbocker was staring about the room, gazing at

29

the women with open effrontery, and a senile leer upon his face. I felt ashamed of him. Yet, oddly enough, no one about us seemed in the least disturbed.

"Now, what cocktail will you have?" said my companion. "There's a new one this week, the Fantan, fifty cents each, will you have that? Right? Two Fantans. Now to eat – what would you like?"

"May I have a slice of cold beef and a pint of ale?"

"Beef!" said Knickerbocker contemptuously. "My dear fellow, you can't have that. Beef is only fifty cents. Do take something reasonable. Try Lobster Newburg, or no, here's a more expensive thing – Filet Bourbon à la something. I don't know what it is, but by gad, sir, it's three dollars a portion anyway."

"All right," I said. "You order the dinner."

Mr. Knickerbocker proceeded to do so, the head-waiter obsequiously at his side, and his long finger indicating on the menu everything that seemed most expensive and that carried the most incomprehensible name. When he had finished he turned to me again.

"Now," he said, "let's talk."

"Tell me," I said, "about the old days and the old times on Broadway."

"Ah, yes," he answered, "the old days – you mean ten years ago before the Winter Garden was opened. We've been going ahead, sir, going ahead. Why, ten years ago there was practically nothing, sir, above Times Square, and look at it now."

I began to realize that Father Knickerbocker, old as he was, had forgotten all the earlier times with which I associated his memory. There was nothing left but the *cabarets*, and the Gardens, the Palm Rooms, and the ukuleles of to-day. Behind that his mind refused to travel.

"Don't you remember," I asked, "the apple orchards and the quiet groves of trees that used to line Broadway long ago?"

"Groves!" he said. "I'll show you a grove, a coconut grove" – here he winked over his wineglass in a senile fashion – "that has apple-trees beaten from here to Honolulu." Thus he babbled on.

All through our meal his talk continued: of *cabarets* and

dances, or fox-trots and midnight suppers, of blondes and brunettes, "peaches" and "dreams," and all the while his eye roved incessantly among the tables, resting on the women with a bold stare. At times he would indicate and point out for me some of what he called the "representative people" present.

"Notice that man at the second table," he would whisper across to me. "He's worth all the way to ten millions: made it in Government contracts; they tried to send him to the penitentiary last fall but they can't get him — he's too smart for them! I'll introduce you to him presently. See the man with him? That's his lawyer, biggest crook in America, they say; we'll meet him after dinner." Then he would suddenly break off and exclaim: "Egad, sir, there's a fine bunch of them," as another bevy of girls came trooping out upon the stage.

"I wonder," I murmured, "if there is nothing left of him but this? Has all the fine old spirit gone? Is it all drowned out in wine and suffocated in the foul atmosphere of luxury?"

Then suddenly I looked up at my companion, and I saw to my surprise that his whole face and manner had altered. His hand was clenched tight on the edge of the table. His eyes looked before him — through and beyond the riotous crowd all about him — into vacancy, into the far past, back into memories that I thought forgotten. His face had altered. The senile, leering look was gone, and in its place the firm-set face of the Knickerbocker of a century ago.

He was speaking in a strange voice, deep and strong.

"Listen," he said, "listen. Do you hear it — there — far out at sea — ships' guns — listen — they're calling for help — ships' guns — far out at sea!" He had clasped me by the arm. "Quick, to the Battery, they'll need every man to-night, they'll —"

Then he sank back into his chair. His look changed again. The vision died out of his eyes.

"What was I saying?" he asked. "Ah, yes, this old brandy, a very special brand. They keep it for me here, a dollar a glass. They *know* me here," he added in his fatuous way. "All the waiters know me. The headwaiter always knows me the minute I come into the room — keeps a chair for me. Now try this brandy and then presently we'll move on and see what's doing at some of the shows."

But somehow, in spite of himself, my companion seemed to be unable to bring himself fully back into the consciousness of the scene before him. The far-away look still lingered in his eyes.

Presently he turned and spoke to me in a low, confidential tone.

"Was I talking to myself a moment ago?" he asked. "Yes? Ah, I feared I was. Do you know – I don't mind telling it to you – lately I've had a strange, queer feeling that comes over me at times, as if *something were happening* – something, I don't know what. I suppose," he continued, with a false attempt at resuming his fatuous manner, "I'm going the pace a little too hard, eh! Makes one fanciful. But the fact is, at times" – he spoke gravely again – "I feel as if there were something happening, something coming."

"Knickerbocker," I said earnestly, "Father Knickerbocker, don't you know that something *is* happening, that this very evening as we are sitting here in all this riot, the President of the United States is to come before Congress on the most solemn mission that ever —"

But my speech fell unheeded. Knickerbocker had picked up his glass again and was leering over it at a bevy of girls dancing upon the stage.

"Look at that girl," he interrupted quickly, "the one dancing at the end. What do you think of her, eh? Some peach!"

Knickerbocker broke off suddenly. For at this moment our ears caught the sound of a noise, a distant tumult, as it were, far down the street and growing nearer. The old man had drawn himself erect in his seat, his hand to his ear, listening as he caught the sound.

"Out on the Broad Way," he said, instinctively calling it by its ancient name as if a flood of memories were upon him. "Do you hear it? Listen – listen – what is it? I've heard that sound before – I've heard every sound on the Broad Way these two centuries back – what is it? I seem to know it!"

The sound and tumult as of running feet and of many voices crying came louder from the street. The people at the tables had turned in their seats to listen. The music of the orchestra had stopped. The waiters had thrown back the heavy curtains from the windows and the people were crowding to them to look out into the street. Knickerbocker had risen in his place, his eyes looked toward the windows, but his gaze was fixed on vacancy as with one who sees a vision passing.

"I know the sound," he cried. "I see it all again. Look, can't you see them? It's Massachusetts soldiers marching South to the war – can't you hear the beating of the drums and the shrill calling of the fife – the regiments from the North, the first to come. I saw them pass, here where we are sitting, sixty years ago —"

Knickerbocker paused a moment, his hand still extended in the air, and then with a great light upon his face he cried:

"I know it now! I know what it meant, the feeling that has haunted me – the sounds I kept hearing – the guns of the ships at sea and the voices calling in distress! I know now. It means, sir, it means —"

But as he spoke a great cry came up from the street and burst in at the doors and windows, echoing in a single word:

WAR! WAR! The message of the President is for WAR!

"War!" cried Father Knickerbocker, rising to his full height, stern and majestic and shouting in a stentorian tone that echoed through the great room. "War! War! To your places, every one of you! Be done with your idle luxury! Out with the glare of your lights! Begone you painted women and worthless men! To your places every man of you! To the Battery! Man the guns! Stand to it, every one of you for the defence of America – for our New York, New York —"

Then, with the sound "New York, New York" still echoing in my ears I woke up. The vision of my dream was gone. I was still on the seat of the car where I had dozed asleep, the book upon my knee. The train had arrived at the depot and the porters were calling into the doorway of the car: "New York! New York!"

All about me was the stir and hubbub of the great depot.

But loud over all it was heard the call of the newsboys crying "WAR! WAR! The President's message is for WAR! Late extra! WAR! WAR!"

And I knew that a great nation had cast aside the bonds of sloth and luxury, and was girding itself to join in the fight for the free democracy of all mankind.

❦ III ❦

The Prophet in Our Midst

THE Eminent Authority looked around at the little group of us seated about him at the club. He was telling us, or beginning to tell us, about the outcome of the war. It was a thing we wanted to know. We were listening attentively. We felt that we were "getting something."

"I doubt very much," he said, "whether Downing Street realizes the enormous power which the Quai d'Orsay has over the Yildiz Kiosk."

"So do I," I said, "what is it?"

But he hardly noticed the interruption.

"You've got to remember," he went on, "that, from the point of view of the Yildiz, the Wilhelmstrasse is just a thing of yesterday."

"Quite so," I said.

"Of course," he added, "the Ballplatz is quite different."

"Altogether different," I admitted.

"And mind you," he said, "the Ballplatz itself can be largely moved from the Quirinal through the Vatican."

"Why of course it can," I agreed, with as much relief in my tone as I could put into it. After all, what simpler way of moving the Ballplatz than that?

The Eminent Authority took another sip at his tea, and looked round at us through his spectacles.

It was I who was taking on myself to do most of the

answering, because it was I who had brought him there and invited the other men to meet him. "He's coming round at five," I had said, "do come and have a cup of tea and meet him. He knows more about the European situation and the probable solution than any other man living." Naturally they came gladly. They wanted to know – as everybody wants to know – how the war will end. They were just ordinary plain men like myself.

I could see that they were a little mystified, perhaps disappointed. They would have liked, just as I would, to ask a few plain questions, such as, can the Italians knock the stuff out of the Austrians? Are the Rumanians getting licked or not? How many submarines has Germany got, anyway? Such questions, in fact, as we are accustomed to put up to one another every day at lunch and to answer out of the morning paper. As it was, we didn't seem to be getting anywhere.

No one spoke. The silence began to be even a little uncomfortable. It was broken by my friend Rapley, who is in wholesale hardware and who has all the intellectual bravery that goes with it. He asked the Authority straight out the question that we all wanted to put.

"Just what do you mean by the Ballplatz? What is the Ballplatz?"

The Authority smiled an engaging smile.

"Precisely," he said, "I see your drift exactly. You say what *is* the Ballplatz? I reply quite frankly that it is almost impossible to answer. Probably one could best define it as the driving power behind the Ausgleich."

"I see," said Rapley.

"Though the plain fact is that ever since the Herzegovinian embroglio the Ballplatz is little more than a counterpoise to the Wilhelmstrasse."

"Ah!" said Rapley.

"Indeed, as everybody knows, the whole relationship of the Ballplatz with the Nevski Prospekt has emanated from the Wilhelmstrasse."

This was a thing which personally I had *not* known. But I said nothing. Neither did the other men. They continued smoking, looking as innocent as they could.

"Don't misunderstand me," said the Authority, "when I

36

speak of the Nevski Prospekt. I am not referring in any way to the Tsarskoe Selo."

"No, no," we all agreed.

"No doubt there were, as we see it plainly now, undercurrents in all directions from the Tsarskoe Selo."

We all seemed to suggest by our attitude that these undercurrents were sucking at our very feet.

"But the Tsarskoe Selo," said the Authority, "is now definitely eliminated."

We were glad of that; we shifted our feet back into attitudes of ease.

I felt that it was time to ask a leading question.

"Do you think," I said, "that Germany will be broken up by the war?"

"You mean Germany in what sense? Are you thinking of Preuszenthum? Are you referring to Junkerismus?"

"No," I said, quite truthfully, "neither of them."

"Ah," said the Authority, "I see; you mean Germany as a Souverantät embodied in a Reichsland."

"That's it," I said.

"Then it's rather hard," said the Eminent Authority, "to answer your question in plain terms. But I'll try. One thing, of course, is *absolutely* certain, Mittel-Europa goes overboard."

"It does, eh?"

"Oh, yes, absolutely. This is the end of Mittel-Europa. I mean to say – here we've had Mittel-Europa, that is, the Mittel-Europa *idea*, as a sort of fantasmus in front of Teutonism ever since Königgrätz."

The Authority looked all round us in that searching way he had. We all tried to look like men seeing a fantasmus and disgusted at it.

"So you see," he went on, "Mittel-Europa is done with."

"I suppose it is," I said. I didn't know just whether to speak with regret or not. I heard Rapley murmur, "I guess so."

"And there is not a doubt," continued the Authority, "that when Mittel-Europa goes, Grossdeutschthum goes with it."

"Oh, sure to," we all murmured.

"Well, then, there you are – what is the result for Germany – why the thing's as plain as a pikestaff – in fact you're driven to it by the sheer logic of the situation – there is only *one* outcome —"

The Authority was speaking very deliberately. He even paused at this point and lighted a cigarette, while we all listened breathlessly. We felt that we had got the thing to a focus at last.

"Only one outcome – a Staatenbund."

"Great heavens," I said, "not a Staatenbund!"

"Undoubtedly," said the Authority, puffing quietly at his cigarette, as if personally he wouldn't lift a finger to stop the Staatenbund if he could, "that's the end of it, a Staatenbund. In other words, we are back where we were before the Vienna Congress!"

At this he chuckled heartily to himself : so the rest of us laughed too : the thing was *too* absurd. But the Authority, who was a man of nice distinctions and genuinely anxious to instruct us, was evidently afraid that he had overstated things a little.

"Mind you," he said, "there'll be *something* left – certainly the Zollverein and either the Ausgleich or something very like it."

All of the men gave a sort of sigh of relief. It was certainly something to have at least a sort of resemblance or appearance of the Ausgleich among us. We felt that we were getting on. One could see that a number of the men were on the brink of asking questions.

"What about Rumania," asked Nelles – he is a banker and interested in government bonds – "is this the end of it?"

"No," said the Authority, "it's not the end of Rumania, but it *is* the end of Rumanian Irridentismus."

That settled Nelles.

"What about the Turks?" asked Rapley.

"The Turks, or rather, I suppose it would be more proper to say, the Osmanli, as that is no doubt what you mean?" Rapley nodded. "Well, speaking personally, I should say that there's no difficulty in a permanent settlement in that quarter. If I were drawing up the terms of a treaty of peace meant to be really lasting I should lay down three absolute bases; the rest needn't matter" – the Authority paused a moment and then proceeded to count off the three conditions of peace on his fingers – "These would be, first, the evacuation of the Sandjak; second, an international guarantee for the Capitulations; and third, for internal matters, an arrangement along the lines of the original firman of Midhat Pasha."

A murmur of complete satisfaction went round the group.

"I don't say," continued the Eminent Authority, "that there wouldn't be other minor matters to adjust; but they would be a mere detail. You ask me, for instance, for a *milice*, or at least a gendarmerie, in the Albanian hinterland; very good, I grant it you at once. You retain, if you like, you abolish the Cypriotic suzerainty of the Porte – all right. These are matters of indifference."

We all assumed a look of utter indifference.

"But what about the Dardanelles? Would you have them fixed so that ships could go through, or not?" asked Rapley.

He is a plain man, not easily put down and liking a plain answer. He got it.

"The Dardanelles," said the Authority, "could easily be denationalized under a quadrilateral guarantee to be made a pars materia of the pactum fœderis."

"That ought to hold them," I murmured.

The Authority felt now that he had pretty well settled the map of Europe. He rose and shook hands with us all around very cordially. We did not try to detain him. We felt that time like his was too valuable to be wasted on things like us.

"Well, I tell you," said Rapley, as we settled back into our chairs when the Great Authority had gone, "my own opinion, boys, is that the United States and England can trim Germany and Austria any day in the week and twice on Sunday."

After which somebody else said:

"I wonder how many of these submarines Germany has, anyway?"

And then we drifted back into the humbler kind of war talk that we have been carrying on for three years.

But later, as we walked home together, Rapley said to me:

"That fellow threw a lot of light on things in Europe, didn't he?"

And I answered:

"Yes."

What liars we all are!

39

❧IV❧

Personal

Adventures

in the

Spirit World

I DO not write what follows with the expectation of convincing or converting anybody. We Spiritualists, or Spiritists – we call ourselves both, or either – never ask anybody to believe us. If they do, well and good. If not, all right. Our attitude simply is that facts are facts. There they are; believe them or not as you like. As I said the other night, in conversation with Aristotle and John Bunyan and George Washington and a few others, why should anybody believe us? Aristotle, I recollect, said that all that he wished was that everybody should know how happy he was; and Washington said that for his part, if people only knew how bright and beautiful it all was where he was, they would willingly, indeed gladly, pay the mere dollar – itself only a nominal fee – that it cost to talk to him. Bunyan, I remember, added that he himself was quite happy.

But, as I say, I never ask anybody to believe me; the more so as I was once an absolute sceptic myself. As I see it now, I was prejudiced. The mere fact that spiritual séances and the services of a medium involved the payment of money condemned the whole thing in my eyes. I did not realize, as I do now, that these *medii*, like anybody else, have got to live; otherwise they would die and become spirits.

Nor would I now place these disclosures before the public

eyes were it not that I think that in the present crisis they will prove of value to the Allied cause.

But let me begin at the beginning. My own conversion to spiritualism came about, like that of so many others, through the more or less casual remark of a Friend.

Noticing me one day gloomy and depressed, this Friend remarked to me:

"Have you any belief in Spiritualism?"

Had it come from anyone else, I should have turned the question aside with a sneer. But it so happens that I owe a great deal of gratitude to this particular Friend. It was he who, at a time when I was so afflicted with rheumatism that I could scarcely leap five feet into the air without pain, said to me one day quite casually: "Have you ever tried pyro for your rheumatism?" One month later I could leap ten feet in the air – had I been able to – without the slightest malaise. The same man, I may add, hearing me one day exclaiming to myself: "Oh, if there were anything that would remove the stains from my clothes!" said to me very simply and quietly: "Have you ever washed them in luxo?" It was he, too, who, noticing a haggard look on my face after breakfast one morning, inquired immediately what I had been eating for breakfast; after which, with a simplicity and directness which I shall never forget, he said: "Why not eat humpo?"

Nor can I ever forget my feeling on another occasion when, hearing me exclaim aloud: "Oh, if there were only something invented for removing the proteins and amygdaloids from a carbonized diet and leaving only the pure nitrogenous life-giving elements!" seized my hand in his, and said in a voice thrilled with emotion: "There is! It has!"

The reader will understand, therefore, that a question, or query, from such a Friend was not to be put lightly aside. When he asked if I believed in Spiritualism I answered with perfect courtesy:

"To be quite frank, I do not."

There was silence between us for a time, and then my Friend said:

"Have you ever given it a trial?"

I paused a moment, as the idea was a novel one.

"No," I answered, "to be quite candid, I have not."

41

Neither of us spoke for perhaps twenty minutes after this, when my Friend said:

"Have you anything against it?"

I thought awhile and then I said:

"Yes, I have."

My Friend remained silent for perhaps half an hour. Then he asked:

"What?"

I meditated for some time. Then I said:

"This – it seems to me that the whole thing is done for money. How utterly unnatural it is to call up the dead – one's great-grandfather, let us say – and pay money for talking to him."

"Precisely," said my Friend without a moment's pause. "I thought so. Now suppose I could bring you into contact with the spirit world through a medium, or through different *medii*, without there being any question of money, other than a merely nominal fee, the money being, as it were, left out of count, and regarded as only, so to speak, nominal, something given merely *pro forma* and *ad interim*. Under these circumstances, will you try the experiment?"

I rose and took my Friend's hand.

"My dear fellow," I said, "I not only will, but I shall."

From this conversation dated my connection with Spiritualism, which has since opened for me a new world.

It would be out of place for me to indicate the particular address or the particular methods employed by the agency to which my Friend introduced me. I am anxious to avoid anything approaching a commercial tinge in what I write. Moreover, their advertisement can be seen along with many others – all, I am sure, just as honourable and just as trustworthy – in the columns of any daily newspaper. As everybody knows, many methods are employed. The tapping of a table, the movement of a ouija board, or the voice of a trance medium, are only a few among the many devices by which the spirits now enter into communication with us. But in my own case the method used was not only simplicity itself, but was so framed as to carry with it the proof of its own genuineness. One had merely to speak into the receiver of a telephone, and the voice of the spirit was heard through the transmitter as in an ordinary telephone conversation.

It was only natural, after the scoffing remark that I had made, that I should begin with my great-grandfather. Nor can I ever forget the peculiar thrill that went through me when I was informed by the head of the agency that a tracer was being sent out for Great-grandfather to call him to the phone.

Great-grandfather – let me do him this justice – was prompt. He was there in three minutes. Whatever his line of business was in the spirit world – and I was never able to learn it – he must have left it immediately and hurried to the telephone. Whatever later dissatisfaction I may have had with Great-grandfather, let me state it fairly and honestly, he is at least a punctual man. Every time I called he came right away without delay. Let those who are inclined to cavil at the methods of the Spiritualists reflect how impossible it would be to secure such punctuality on anything but a basis of absolute honesty.

In my first conversation with Great-grandfather, I found myself so absurdly nervous at the thought of the vast gulf of space and time across which we were speaking that I perhaps framed my questions somewhat too crudely.

"How are you, great-grandfather?" I asked.

His voice came back to me as distinctly as if he were in the next room:

"I am happy, very happy. Please tell everybody that I am *happy*."

"Great-grandfather," I said. "I will. I'll see that everybody knows it. Where are you, great-grandfather?"

"Here," he answered, "beyond."

"Beyond what?"

"Here on the other side."

"Side of which?" I asked.

"Of the great vastness," he answered. "The other end of the Illimitable."

"Oh, I see," I said, "that's where you are."

We were silent for some time. It is amazing how difficult it is to find things to talk about with one's great-grandfather. For the life of me I could think of nothing better than:

"What sort of weather have you been having?"

"There is no weather here," said Great-grandfather. "It's all bright and beautiful all the time."

"You mean bright sunshine?" I said.

43

"There is no sun here," said Great-grandfather.

"Then how do you mean —" I began.

But at this moment the head of the agency tapped me on the shoulder to remind me that the two minutes' conversation for which I had deposited, as a nominal fee, five dollars, had expired. The agency was courteous enough to inform me that for five dollars more Great-grandfather would talk another two minutes.

But I thought it preferable to stop for the moment.

Now I do not wish to say a word against my own great-grandfather. Yet in the conversations which followed on successive days I found him — how shall I put it? — unsatisfactory. He had been, when on this side — to use the term we Spiritualists prefer — a singularly able man, an English judge; so at least I have always been given to understand. But somehow Great-grandfather's brain, on the other side, seemed to have got badly damaged. My own theory is that, living always in the bright sunshine, he had got sunstroke. But I may wrong him. Perhaps it was locomotor ataxy that he had. That he was very, very happy where he was is beyond all doubt. He said so at every conversation. But I have noticed that feeble-minded people are often happy. He said, too, that he was glad to be where he was; and on the whole I felt glad that he was too. Once or twice I thought that possibly Great-grandfather felt so happy because he had been drinking : his voice, even across the great gulf, seemed somehow to suggest it. But on being questioned he told me that where he was there was no drink and no thirst, because it was all so bright and beautiful. I asked him if he meant that it was "bone-dry" like Kansas, or whether the rich could still get it? But he didn't answer.

Our intercourse ended in a quarrel. No doubt it was my fault. But it *did* seem to me that Great-grandfather, who had been one of the greatest English lawyers of his day, might have handed out an opinion.

The matter came up thus : I had had an argument — it was in the middle of last winter — with some men at my club about the legal interpretation of the Adamson Law. The dispute grew bitter.

"I'm right," I said, "and I'll prove it if you give me time to consult the authorities.'

"Consult your great-grandfather!" sneered one of the men.

"All right," I said, "I will."

I walked straight across the room to the telephone and called up the agency.

"Give me my great-grandfather," I said. "I want him right away."

He was there. Good, punctual old soul, I'll say that for him. He was there.

"Great-grandfather," I said, "I'm in a discussion here about the constitutionality of the Adamson Law, involving the power of Congress under the Constitution. Now, you remember the Constitution when they made it. Is the law all right?"

There was silence.

"How does it stand, great-grandfather?" I said. "Will it hold water?"

Then he spoke.

"Over here," he said, "there are no laws, no members of Congress and no Adamsons; it's all bright and beautiful and —"

"Great-grandfather," I said, as I hung up the receiver in disgust, "you are a Mutt!"

I never spoke to him again. Yet I feel sorry for him, feeble old soul, flitting about in the Illimitable, and always so punctual to hurry to the telephone, so happy, so feeble-witted and courteous; a better man, perhaps, take it all in all, than he was in life; lonely, too, it may be, out there in the Vastness. Yet I never called him up again. He is happy. Let him stay.

Indeed, my acquaintance with the spirit world might have ended at that point but for the good offices, once more, of my Friend.

"You find your great-grandfather a little slow, a little dull?" he said. "Well, then, if you want brains, power, energy, why not call up some of the spirits of the great men, some of the leading men, for instance, of your great-grandfather's time?"

"You've said it!" I exclaimed. "I'll call up Napoleon Bonaparte."

I hurried to the agency.

"Is it possible," I asked, "for me to call up the Emperor Napoleon and talk to him?"

Possible? Certainly. It appeared that nothing was easier. In the case of Napoleon Bonaparte the nominal fee had to be ten dollars in place of five; but it seemed to me that, if Great-grandfather cost five, Napoleon Bonaparte at ten was cheapness itself.

"Will it take long to get him?" I asked anxiously.

"We'll send out a tracer for him right away," they said.

Like Great-grandfather, Napoleon was punctual. That I will say for him. If in any way I think less of Napoleon Bonaparte now than I did, let me at least admit that a more punctual, obliging, willing man I never talked with.

He came in two minutes.

"He's on the line now," they said.

I took up the receiver, trembling.

"Hello!" I called. "Est-ce que c'est l'Empereur Napoléon à qui j'ai l'honneur de parler?"

"How's that?" said Napoleon.

"Je demande si je suis en communication avec l'Empereur Napoléon —"

"Oh," said Napoleon, "that's all right; speak English."

"What!" I said in surprise. "You know English? I always thought you couldn't speak a word of it."

He was silent for a minute. Then he said:

"I picked it up over here. It's all right. Go right ahead."

"Well," I continued, "I've always admired you so much, your wonderful brain and genius, that I felt I wanted to speak to you and ask you how you are."

"Happy," said Napoleon, "very happy."

"That's good," I said. "That's fine! And how is it out there? All bright and beautiful, eh?"

"Very beautiful," said the Emperor.

"And just where are you?" I continued. "Somewhere out in the Unspeakable, I suppose, eh?"

"Yes," he answered, "out here beyond."

"That's good," I said. "Pretty happy, eh?"

"Very happy," said Napoleon. "Tell everybody how happy I am."

"I know," I answered. "I'll tell them all. But just now I've a particular thing to ask. We've got a big war on, pretty well the whole world in it, and I thought perhaps a few pointers from a man like you —"

But at this point the attendant touched me on the shoulder. "Your time is up," he said.

I was about to offer to pay at once for two minutes more when a better idea struck me. Talk with Napoleon? I'd do better than that. I'd call a whole War Council of great spirits, lay the war crisis before them and get the biggest brains that the world ever produced to work on how to win the war.

Who should I have? Let me see! Napoleon himself, of course. I'd bring him back. And for the sea business, the submarine problem, I'd have Nelson. George Washington, naturally, for the American end; for politics, say, good old Ben Franklin, the wisest old head that ever walked on American legs, and witty too; yes, Franklin certainly, if only for his wit to keep the council from getting gloomy; Lincoln – honest old Abe – him certainly I must have. Those and perhaps a few others.

I reckoned that a consultation at ten dollars apiece with spirits of that class was cheap to the verge of the ludicrous. Their advice ought to be worth millions – yes, billions – to the cause.

The agency got them for me without trouble. There is no doubt they are a punctual crowd, over there beyond in the Unthinkable.

I gathered them all in and talked to them, all and severally, the payment, a merely nominal matter, being made, *pro forma*, in advance.

I have in front of me in my rough notes the result of their advice. When properly drafted it will be, I feel sure, one of the most important state documents produced in the war.

In the personal sense – I have to admit it – I found them just a trifle disappointing. Franklin, poor fellow, has apparently lost his wit. The spirit of Lincoln seemed to me to have none of that homely wisdom that he used to have. And it appears that we were quite mistaken in thinking Disraeli a brilliant man; it is clear to me now that he was dull – just about as dull as Great-grandfather, I should say. Washington, too, is not at all the kind of man we thought him.

Still, these are only personal impressions. They detract nothing from the extraordinary value of the advice given, which seems to me to settle once and for ever any lingering

47

doubt about the value of communications with the Other Side.

My draft of their advice runs in part as follows:

The Spirit of Nelson, on being questioned on the submarine problem, holds that if all the men on the submarines were where he is everything would be bright and happy. This seems to me an invaluable hint. There is nothing needed now except to put them there.

The advice of the Spirit of Napoleon about the campaign on land seemed to me, if possible, of lower value than that of Nelson on the campaign at sea. It is hardly conceivable that Napoleon has forgotten where the Marne is. But it may have changed since his day. At any rate, he says that, if ever the Russians cross the Marne, all is over. Coming from such a master-strategist, this ought to be attended to.

Franklin, on being asked whether the United States had done right in going into the war, said "Yes"; asked whether the country could with honour have stayed out, he said "No." There is guidance here for thinking men of all ranks.

Lincoln is very happy where he is. So, too, I was amazed to find, is Disraeli. In fact, it was most gratifying to learn that all of the great spirits consulted are very happy, and want everybody to know how happy they are. Where they are, I may say, it is all bright and beautiful.

Fear of trespassing on their time prevented me from questioning each of them up to the full limit of the period contracted for.

I understand that I have still to my credit at the agency five minutes' talk with Napoleon, available at any time, and similarly five minutes each with Franklin and Washington, to say nothing of ten minutes' unexpired time with Great-grandfather.

All of these opportunities I am willing to dispose of at a reduced rate to anyone still sceptical of the reality of the spirit world.

V

The Sorrows
of a
Summer Guest

LET me admit, as I start to write, that the whole thing is my own fault. I should never have come. I knew better. I have known better for years. I have known that it is sheer madness to go and pay visits in other people's houses.

Yet in a moment of insanity I have let myself in for it and here I am. There is no hope, no outlet now till the first of September when my visit is to terminate. Either that or death. I do not greatly care which.

I write this, where no human eye can see me, down by the pond – they call it the lake – at the foot of Beverly-Jones's estate. It is six o'clock in the morning. No one is up. For a brief hour or so there is peace. But presently Miss Larkspur – the jolly English girl who arrived last week – will throw open her casement window and call across the lawn, "Hullo everybody! What a ripping morning!" And young Popple-son will call back in a Swiss yodel from somewhere in the shrubbery, and Beverly-Jones will appear on the piazza with big towels round his neck and shout, "Who's coming for an early dip?" And so the day's fun and jollity – heaven help me – will begin again.

Presently they will all come trooping in to breakfast, in coloured blazers and fancy blouses, laughing and grabbing at the food with mimic rudeness and bursts of hilarity. And to think that I might have been breakfasting at my club with

49

the morning paper propped against the coffee-pot, in a silent room in the quiet of the city.

I repeat that it is my own fault that I am here.

For many years it had been a principle of my life to visit nobody. I had long since learned that visiting only brings misery. If I got a card or telegram that said, "Won't you run up to the Adirondacks and spend the week-end with us?" I sent back word: "No, not unless the Adirondacks can run faster than I can," or words to that effect. If the owner of a country house wrote to me: "Our man will meet you with a trap any afternoon that you care to name," I answered, in spirit at least: "No, he won't, not unless he has a bear-trap or one of those traps in which they catch wild antelope." If any fashionable lady friend wrote to me in the peculiar jargon that they use: "Can you give us from July the twelfth at half-after-three till the fourteenth at four?" I replied: "Madam, take the whole month, take a year, but leave me in peace."

Such at least was the spirit of my answers to invitations. In practice I used to find it sufficient to send a telegram that read: "Crushed with work impossible to get away," and then stroll back into the reading-room of the club and fall asleep again.

But my coming here was my own fault. It resulted from one of those unhappy moments of expansiveness such as occur, I imagine, to everybody – moments when one appears to be something quite different from what one really is, when one feels oneself a thorough good fellow, sociable, merry, appreciative, and finds the people around one the same. Such moods are known to all of us. Some people say that it is the super-self asserting itself. Others say it is from drinking. But let it pass. That at any rate was the kind of mood that I was in when I met Beverly-Jones and when he asked me here.

It was in the afternoon, at the club. As I recall it, we were drinking cocktails and I was thinking what a bright, genial fellow Beverly-Jones was, and how completely I had mistaken him. For myself – I admit it – I am a brighter, better man after drinking two cocktails than at any other time – quicker, kindlier, more genial. And higher, morally. I had been telling stories in that inimitable way that one has after two cocktails. In reality, I only know four stories, and a fifth that I don't quite remember, but in moments of expansiveness they feel like a fund or flow.

It was under such circumstances that I sat with Beverly-Jones. And it was in shaking hands at leaving that he said: "I *do* wish, old chap, that you could run up to our summer place and give us the whole of August!" and I answered, as I shook him warmly by the hand: "My *dear* fellow, I'd simply *love* to!" "By gad, then it's a go!" he said. "You must come up for August, and wake us all up!"

Wake them up! Ye gods! Me wake them up!

One hour later I was repenting of my folly, and wishing, when I thought of the two cocktails, that the prohibition wave could be hurried up so as to leave us all high and dry — bone-dry, silent and unsociable.

Then I clung to the hope that Beverly-Jones would forget. But no. In due time his wife wrote to me. They were looking forward so much, she said, to my visit; they felt — she repeated her husband's ominous phrase — that I should wake them all up!

What sort of alarm-clock did they take me for, anyway!

Ah, well! They know better now. It was only yesterday afternoon that Beverly-Jones found me standing here in the gloom of some cedar-trees beside the edge of the pond and took me back so quietly to the house that I realized he thought I meant to drown myself. So I did.

I could have stood it better — my coming here, I mean — if they hadn't come down to the station in a body to meet me in one of those long vehicles with seats down the sides: silly-looking men in coloured blazers and girls with no hats, all making a hullabaloo of welcome. "We are quite a small party," Mrs. Beverly-Jones had written. Small! Great heavens, what would they call a large one? And even those at the station turned out to be only half of them. There were just as many more all lined up on the piazza of the house as we drove up, all waving a fool welcome with tennis rackets and golf clubs.

Small party, indeed! Why, after six days there are still some of the idiots whose names I haven't got straight! That fool with the fluffy moustache, which is he? And that jackass that made the salad at the picnic yesterday, is he the brother of the woman with the guitar, or who?

51

But what I mean is, there is something in that sort of noisy welcome that puts me to the bad at the start. It always does. A group of strangers all laughing together, and with a set of catchwords and jokes all their own, always throws me into a fit of sadness, deeper than words. I had thought, when Mrs. Beverly-Jones said a *small* party, she really meant small. I had had a mental picture of a few sad people, greeting me very quietly and gently, and of myself, quiet, too, but cheerful – somehow lifting them up, with no great effort, by my mere presence.

Somehow from the very first I could feel that Beverly-Jones was disappointed in me. He said nothing. But I knew it. On that first afternoon, between my arrival and dinner, he took me about his place, to show it to me. I wish that at some proper time I had learned just what it is that you say when a man shows you about his place. I never knew before how deficient I am in it. I am all right to be shown an iron-and-steel plant, or a soda-water factory, or anything really wonderful, but being shown a house and grounds and trees, things that I have seen all my life, leaves me absolutely silent.

"These big gates," said Beverly-Jones, "we only put up this year."

"Oh," I said. That was all. Why shouldn't they put them up this year? I didn't care if they'd put them up this year or a thousand years ago.

"We had quite a struggle," he continued, "before we finally decided on sandstone.

"You did, eh?" I said. There seemed nothing more to say; I didn't know what sort of struggle he meant, or who fought who; and personally sandstone or soapstone or any other stone is all the same to me.

"This lawn," said Beverly-Jones, "we laid down the first year we were here." I answered nothing. He looked me right in the face as he said it and I looked straight back at him, but I saw no reason to challenge his statement. "The geraniums along the border," he went on, "are rather an experiment. They're Dutch."

I looked fixedly at the geraniums but never said a word. They were Dutch; all right, why not? They were an experiment. Very good; let them be so. I know nothing in particular to say about a Dutch experiment.

I could feel that Beverly-Jones grew depressed as he showed me round. I was sorry for him, but unable to help. I realized that there were certain sections of my education that had been neglected. How to be shown things and make appropriate comments seems to be an art in itself. I don't possess it. It is not likely now, as I look at this pond, that I ever shall.

Yet how simple a thing it seems when done by others. I saw the difference at once the very next day, the second day of my visit, when Beverly-Jones took round young Poppleton, the man that I mentioned above who will presently give a Swiss yodel from a clump of laurel bushes to indicate that the day's fun has begun.

Poppleton I had known before slightly. I used to see him at the club. In club surroundings he always struck me as an ineffable young ass, loud and talkative and perpetually breaking the silence rules. Yet I have to admit that in his summer flannels and with a straw hat on he can do things that I can't.

"These big gates," began Beverly-Jones as he showed Poppleton round the place with me trailing beside them, "we only put up this year."

Poppleton, who has a summer place of his own, looked at the gates very critically.

"Now, do you know what I'd have done with those gates, if they were mine?" he said.

"No," said Beverly-Jones.

"I'd have set them two feet wider apart; they're too narrow, old chap, too narrow." Poppleton shook his head sadly at the gates.

"We had quite a struggle," said Beverly-Jones, "before we finally decided on sandstone "

I realized that he had one and the same line of talk that he always used. I resented it. No wonder it was easy for him.

"Great mistake," said Poppleton. "Too soft. Look at this" — here he picked up a big stone and began pounding at the gate-post — "see how easily it chips! Smashes right off. Look at that, the whole corner knocks right off, see!"

Beverly-Jones entered no protest. I began to see that there is a sort of understanding, a kind of freemasonry, among men who have summer places. One shows his things; the other runs them down, and smashes them. This makes the whole thing easy at once. Beverly-Jones showed his lawn.

"Your turf is all wrong, old boy," said Poppleton. "Look! it has no body to it. See, I can kick holes in it with my heel. Look at that, and that! If I had on stronger boots I could kick this lawn all to pieces."

"These geraniums along the border," said Beverly-Jones, "are rather an experiment. They're Dutch."

"But my dear fellow," said Poppleton, "you've got them set in wrongly. They ought to slope *from* the sun you know, never *to* it. Wait a bit" – here he picked up a spade that was lying where a gardener had been working – "I'll throw a few out. Notice how easily they come up. Ah, that fellow broke! They're apt to. There, I won't bother to reset them, but tell your man to slope them over from the sun. That's the idea."

Beverly-Jones showed his new boat-house next and Poppleton knocked a hole in the side with a hammer to show that the lumber was too thin.

"If that were *my* boat-house," he said, "I'd rip the outside clean off it and use shingle and stucco."

It was, I noticed, Poppleton's plan first to imagine Beverly-Jones's things his own, and then to smash them, and then give them back smashed to Beverly-Jones. This seemed to please them both. Apparently it is a well-understood method of entertaining a guest and being entertained. Beverly-Jones and Poppleton, after an hour or so of it, were delighted with one another.

Yet somehow, when I tried it myself, it failed to work.

"Do you know what I would do with that cedar summer-house if it was mine?" I asked my host the next day.

"No," he said.

"I'd knock the thing down and burn it," I answered.

But I think I must have said it too fiercely. Beverly-Jones looked hurt and said nothing.

Not that these people are not doing all they can for me. I know that. I admit it. If I *should* meet my end here and if – to put the thing straight out – my lifeless body is found floating on the surface of this pond, I should like there to be documentary evidence of *that* much. They are trying their best. "This is Liberty Hall," Mrs. Beverly-Jones said to me on the first day of my visit. "We want you to feel that you are to do absolutely as you like!"

Absolutely as I like! How little they know me. I should like to have answered: "Madam, I have now reached a time of life when human society at breakfast is impossible to me; when any conversation prior to eleven a.m. must be considered out of the question; when I prefer to eat my meals in quiet, or with such mild hilarity as can be got from a comic paper; when I can no longer wear nankeen pants and a coloured blazer without a sense of personal indignity; when I can no longer leap and play in the water like a young fish; when I do not yodel, cannot sing and, to my regret, dance even worse than I did when young; and when the mood of mirth and hilarity comes to me only as a rare visitant – shall we say at a burlesque performance – and never as a daily part of my existence. Madam, I am unfit to be a summer guest. If this is Liberty Hall indeed, let me, oh, let me go!"

Such is the speech that I would make if it were possible. As it is, I can only rehearse it to myself.

Indeed, the more I analyse it the more impossible it seems, for a man of my temperament at any rate, to be a summer guest. These people, and, I imagine, all other summer people, seem to be trying to live in a perpetual joke. Everything, all day, has to be taken in a mood of uproarious fun.

However, I can speak of it all now in quiet retrospect and without bitterness. It will soon be over now. Indeed, the reason why I have come down at this early hour to this quiet water is that things have reached a crisis. The situation has become extreme and I must end it.

It happened last night. Beverly-Jones took me aside while the others were dancing the fox-trot to the victrola on the piazza.

"We're planning to have some rather good fun to-morrow night," he said, "something that will be a good deal more in your line than a lot of it, I'm afraid, has been up here. In fact, my wife says that this will be the very thing for you."

"Oh," I said.

"We're going to get all the people from the other houses over and the girls" – this term Beverly-Jones uses to mean his wife and her friends – "are going to get up a sort of entertainment with charades and things, all impromptu, more or less, of course —".

"Oh," I said. I saw already what was coming.

"And they want you to act as a sort of master-of-ceremonies, to make up the gags and introduce the different stunts and all that. I was telling the girls about that afternoon at the club, when you were simply killing us all with those funny stories of yours, and they're all wild over it."

"Wild?" I repeated.

"Yes, quite wild over it. They say it will be the hit of the summer."

Beverly-Jones shook hands with great warmth as we parted for the night. I knew that he was thinking that my character was about to be triumphantly vindicated, and that he was glad for my sake.

Last night I did not sleep. I remained awake all night thinking of the "entertainment." In my whole life I have done nothing in public except once when I presented a walking-stick to the vice-president of our club on the occasion of his taking a trip to Europe. Even for that I used to rehearse to myself far into the night sentences that began: "This walking-stick, gentleman, means far more than a mere walking-stick."

And now they expect me to come out as a merry master-of-ceremonies before an assembled crowd of summer guests.

But never mind. It is nearly over now. I have come down to this quiet water in the early morning to throw myself in. They will find me floating here among the lilies. Some few will understand. I can see it written, as it will be, in the newspapers.

"What makes the sad fatality doubly poignant is that the unhappy victim had just entered upon a holiday visit that was to have been prolonged throughout the whole month. Needless to say, he was regarded as the life and soul of the pleasant party of holiday makers that had gathered at the delightful country home of Mr. and Mrs. Beverly-Jones. Indeed, on the very day of the tragedy, he was to have taken a leading part in staging a merry performance of charades and parlour entertainments – a thing for which his genial talents and overflowing high spirits rendered him specially fit."

When they read that, those who know me best will understand how and why I died. "He had still over three weeks to stay there," they will say. "He was to act as the stage manager of charades." They will shake their heads. They will understand.

But what is this? I raise my eyes from the paper and I see Beverly-Jones hurriedly approaching from the house. He is hastily dressed, with flannel trousers and a dressing-gown. His face looks grave. Something has happened. Thank God, something has happened. Some accident! Some tragedy! Something to prevent the charades!

I write these few lines on a fast train that is carrying me back to New York, a cool, comfortable train, with a deserted club-car where I can sit in a leather arm-chair, with my feet up on another, smoking, silent, and at peace.

Villages, farms and summer places are flying by. Let them fly. I, too, am flying – back to the rest and quiet of the city.

"Old man," Beverly-Jones said, as he laid his hand on mine very kindly – he is a decent fellow, after all, is Jones – "they're calling you by long-distance from New York."

"What is it?" I asked, or tried to gasp.

"It's bad news, old chap; fire in your office last evening. I'm afraid a lot of your private papers were burned. Robinson – that's your senior clerk, isn't it? – seems to have been on the spot trying to save things. He's badly singed about the face and hands. I'm afraid you must go at once."

"Yes, yes," I said, "at once."

"I know. I've told the man to get the trap ready right away. You've just time to catch the seven-ten. Come along."

"Right," I said. I kept my face as well as I could, trying to hide my exultation. The office burnt! Fine! Robinson's singed! Glorious! I hurriedly packed my things and whispered to Beverly-Jones farewell messages for the sleeping household. I never felt so jolly and facetious in my life. I could feel that Beverly-Jones was admiring the spirit and pluck with which I took my misfortune. Later on he would tell them all about it.

The trap ready! Hurrah! Good-bye, old man! Hurrah! All right. I'll telegraph. Right you are, good-bye. Hip, hip, hurrah! Here we are! Train right on time. Just these two bags, porter, and there's a dollar for you. What merry, merry fellows these darky porters are, anyway!

And so here I am in the train, safe bound for home and the summer quiet of my club.

Well done for Robinson! I was afraid that it had missed fire, or that my message to him had gone wrong. It was on the second day of my visit that I sent word to him to invent an accident — something, anything — to call me back. I thought the message had failed. I had lost hope. But it is all right now, though he certainly pitched the note pretty high.

Of course I can't let the Beverly-Joneses know that it was a put-up job. I must set fire to the office as soon as I get back. But it's worth it. And I'll have to singe Robinson about the face and hands. But it's worth that too!

⚜ VI ⚜

To Nature
and
Back Again

IT WAS probably owing to the fact that my place of lodgment in New York overlooked the waving trees of Central Park that I was consumed, all the summer through, with a great longing for the woods. To me, as a lover of Nature, the waving of a tree conveys thoughts which are never conveyed to me except by seeing a tree wave.

This longing grew upon me. I became restless with it. In the daytime I dreamed over my work. At night my sleep was broken and restless. At times I would even wander forth at night into the park, and there, deep in the night shadow of the trees, imagine myself alone in the recesses of the dark woods remote from the toil and fret of our distracted civilization.

This increasing feeling culminated in the resolve which becomes the subject of this narrative. The thought came to me suddenly one night. I woke from my sleep with a plan fully matured in my mind. It was this: I would, for one month, cast off all the travail and cares of civilized life and become again the wild man of the woods that Nature made me. My plan was to go to the edge of the great woods, somewhere in New England, divest myself of my clothes – except only my union suit – crawl into the woods, stay there a month and then crawl out again. To a trained woodsman and crawler like myself the thing was simplicity itself. For food

I knew that I could rely on berries, roots, shoots, mosses, mushrooms, fungi, bungi – in fact the whole of Nature's ample storehouse; for my drink, the running brook and the quiet pool; and for my companions the twittering chipmunk, the chickadee, the chocktaw, the choo-choo, the chow-chow, and the hundred and one inhabitants of the forgotten glade and the tangled thicket.

Fortunately for me, my resolve came to me upon the last day in August. The month of September was my vacation. My time was my own. I was free to go.

On my rising in the morning my preparations were soon made; or, rather, there were practically no preparations to make. I had but to supply myself with a camera, my one necessity in the woods, and to say good-bye to my friends. Even this last ordeal I wished to make as brief as possible. I had no wish to arouse their anxiety over the dangerous, perhaps foolhardy, project that I had in mind. I wished, as far as possible, to say good-bye in such a way as to allay the very natural fears which my undertaking would excite in the minds of my friends.

From myself, although trained in the craft of the woods, I could not conceal the danger that I incurred. Yet the danger was almost forgotten in the extraordinary and novel interest that attached to the experiment. Would it prove possible for a man, unaided by our civilized arts and industries, to maintain himself naked – except for his union suit – in the heart of the woods? Could he do it, or could he not? And if he couldn't what then?

But this last thought I put from me. Time alone could answer the question.

As in duty bound, I went first to the place of business where I am employed, to shake hands and say good-bye to my employer.

"I am going," I said, "to spend a month naked alone in the woods."

He looked up from his desk with genial kindliness.

"That's right," he said, "get a good rest."

"My plan is," I added, "to live on berries and funguses."

"Fine," he answered. "Well, have a good time, old man – good-bye."

Then I dropped in casually upon one of my friends.

"Well," I said, "I'm off to New England to spend a month naked."

"Nantucket," he said, "or Newport?"

"No," I answered, speaking as lightly as I could. "I'm going into the woods and stay there naked for a month."

"Oh, yes," he said. "I see. Well, good-bye, old chap — see you when you get back."

After that I called upon two or three other men to say a brief word of farewell. I could not help feeling slightly nettled, I must confess, at the very casual way in which they seemed to take my announcement. "Oh, yes," they said, "naked in the woods, eh? Well, ta-ta till you get back."

Here was a man about to risk his life — for there was no denying the fact — in a great sociological experiment, yet they received the announcement with absolute unconcern. It offered one more assurance, had I needed it, of the degenerate state of the civilization upon which I was turning my back.

On my way to the train I happened to run into a newspaper reporter with whom I have some acquaintance.

"I'm just off," I said, "to New England to spend a month naked — at least naked all but my union suit — in the woods; no doubt you'll like a few details about it for your paper."

"Thanks, old man," he said, "we've pretty well given up running that nature stuff. We couldn't do anything with it — unless, of course, anything happens to you. Then we'd be glad to give you some space."

Several of my friends had at least the decency to see me off on the train. One, and one alone accompanied me on the long night-ride to New England in order that he might bring back my clothes, my watch, and other possessions from the point where I should enter the woods, together with such few messages of farewell as I might scribble at the last moment.

It was early morning when we arrived at the wayside station where we were to alight. From here we walked to the edge of the woods. Arrived at this point we halted. I took off my clothes, with the exception of my union suit. Then, taking a pot of brown stain from my valise, I proceeded to dye my face and hands and my union suit itself a deep butternut brown.

61

"What's that for?" asked my friend.

"For protection," I answered. "Don't you know that all animals are protected by their peculiar markings that render them invisible? The caterpillar looks like the leaf it eats from; the scales of the fish counterfeit the glistening water of the brook; the bear and the 'possum are coloured like the tree-trunks on which they climb. There!" I added, as I concluded my task. "I am now invisible."

"Gee!" said my friend.

I handed him back the valise and the empty paint-pot, dropped to my hands and knees – my camera slung about my neck – and proceeded to crawl into the bush. My friend stood watching me.

"Why don't you stand up and walk?" I heard him call.

I turned half round and growled at him. Then I plunged deeper into the bush, growling as I went.

After ten minutes' active crawling I found myself in the heart of the forest. It reached all about me on every side for hundreds of miles. All around me was the unbroken stillness of the woods. Not a sound reached my ear save the twittering of a squirrel, or squirl, in the branches high above my head, or the far-distant call of a loon hovering over some woodland lake.

I judged that I had reached a spot suitable for my habitation.

My first care was to make a fire. Difficult though it might appear to the degenerate dweller of the city to do this, to the trained woodsman, such as I had now become, it is nothing. I selected a dry stick, rubbed it vigorously against my hind leg, and in a few moments it broke into a generous blaze. Half an hour later I was sitting beside a glowing fire of twigs discussing with great gusto an appetizing mess of boiled grass and fungi cooked in a hollow stone.

I ate my fill, not pausing till I was full, careless, as the natural man ever is, of the morrow. Then, stretched out upon the pine-needles at the foot of a great tree, I lay in drowsy contentment listening to the song of the birds, the hum of the myriad insects and the strident note of the squirrel high above me. At times I would give utterance to the soft answering call, known to every woodsman, that is part of the freemasonry of animal speech. As I lay thus, I would not have exchanged places with the pale dweller in the city for all the wealth in the world. Here I lay remote from the world, happy, full of grass, listening to the crooning of the birds.

But the mood of inaction and reflection cannot last, even with the lover of Nature. It was time to be up and doing. Much lay before me to be done before the setting of the sun should bring with it, as I fully expected it would, darkness. Before night fell I must build a house, make myself a suit of clothes, lay in a store of nuts, and in short prepare myself for the oncoming of winter, which, in the bush, may come on at any time in the summer.

I rose briskly from the ground to my hands and knees and set myself to the building of my house. The method that I intended to follow here was merely that which Nature has long since taught to the beaver and which, moreover, is known and practised by the gauchos of the pampas, by the googoos of Rhodesia and by many other tribes. I had but to select a suitable growth of trees and gnaw them down with my teeth, taking care so to gnaw them that each should fall into the place appointed for it in the building. The sides, once erected in this fashion, another row of trees, properly situated, is gnawed down to fall crosswise as the roof.

I set myself briskly to work and in half an hour had already the satisfaction of seeing my habitation rising into shape. I was still gnawing with unabated energy when I was interrupted by a low growling in the underbrush. With animal caution I shrank behind a tree, growling in return. I could see something moving in the bushes, evidently an animal of large size. From its snarl I judged it to be a bear. I could hear it moving nearer to me. It was about to attack me. A savage joy thrilled through me at the thought, while my union suit bristled with rage from head to foot as I emitted growl after growl of defiance. I bared my teeth to the gums, snarling, and lashed my flank with my hind foot. Eagerly I watched for the onrush of the bear. In savage combat who strikes first wins. It was my idea, as soon as the bear should appear, to bite off its front legs one after the other. This initial advantage once gained, I had no doubt of ultimate victory.

The brushes parted. I caught a glimpse of a long brown

body and a hairy head. Then the creature reared up, breasting itself against a log, full in front of me. Great heavens! It was not a bear at all. It was a man.

He was dressed, as I was, in a union suit, and his face and hands, like mine were stained a butternut brown. His hair was long and matted and two weeks' stubble of beard was on his face.

For a minute we both glared at one another, still growling. Then the man rose up to a standing position with a muttered exclamation of disgust.

"Ah, cut it out," he said. "Let's talk English."

He walked over towards me and sat down upon a log in an attitude that seemed to convey the same disgust as the expression of his features. Then he looked round about him.

"What are you doing?" he said.

"Building a house," I answered.

"I know," he said with a nod. "What are you here for?"

"Why," I explained, "my plan is this: I want to see whether a man can come out here in the woods, naked, with no aid but that of his own hands and his own ingenuity and —"

"Yes, yes, I know," interrupted the disconsolate man. "Earn himself a livelihood in the wilderness, live as the cave-man lived, carefree and far from the curse of civilization!"

"That's it. That was my idea," I said, my enthusiasm rekindling as I spoke. "That's what I'm doing; my food is to be the rude grass and the roots that Nature furnishes for her children, and for my drink —"

"Yes, yes," he interrupted again with impatience, "for your drink the running rill, for your bed the sweet couch of hemlock, and for your canopy the open sky lit with the soft stars in the deep-purple vault of the dewy night. I know."

"Great heavens, man!" I exclaimed. "That's my idea exactly. In fact, those are my very phrases. How could you have guessed it?"

He made a gesture with his hand to indicate weariness and disillusionment.

"Pshaw!" he said. "I know it because I've been doing it. I've been here a fortnight now on this open-air, life-in-the-woods game. Well, I'm sick of it! This last lets me out."

"What last?" I asked.

"Why, meeting you. Do you realize that you are the nineteenth man that I've met in the last three days running about naked in the woods? They're all doing it. The woods are full of them."

"You don't say so!" I gasped.

"Fact. Wherever you go in the bush you find naked men all working out this same blasted old experiment. Why, when you get a little farther in you'll see signs up: NAKED MEN NOT ALLOWED IN THIS BUSH, and NAKED MEN KEEP OFF, and GENTLEMEN WHO ARE NAKED WILL KINDLY KEEP TO THE HIGH ROAD, and a lot of things like that. You must have come in at a wrong place or you'd have noticed the little shanties that they have now at the edge of the New England bush with signs up: UNION SUITS BOUGHT AND SOLD, CAMERAS FOR SALE OR TO RENT, HIGHEST PRICE FOR CAST-OFF CLOTHING, and all that sort of thing."

"No," I said. "I saw nothing."

"Well, you look when you go back. As for me, I'm done with it. The thing's worked out. I'm going back to the city to see whether I can't, right there in the heart of the city, earn myself a livelihood with my unaided hands and brains. That's the real problem; no more bumming on the animals for me. This bush business is too easy. Well, good-bye; I'm off."

"But stop a minute," I said. "How is it that, if what you say is true, I haven't seen or heard anybody in the bush, and I've been here since the middle of the morning?"

"Nonsense," the man answered. "They were probably all round you but you didn't recognize them."

"No, no, it's not possible. I lay here dreaming beneath a tree and there wasn't a sound, except the twittering of a squirrel and, far away, the cry of a lake-loon, nothing else."

"Exactly, the twittering of a squirrel! That was some feller up the tree twittering to beat the band to let on that he was a squirrel, and no doubt some other feller calling out like a loon over near the lake. I suppose you gave them the answering cry?"

"I did," I said. "I gave that low guttural note which —"

"Precisely — which is the universal greeting in the freemasonry of animal speech. I see you've got it all down pat. Well, good-bye again. I'm off. Oh, don't bother to growl, please. I'm sick of that line of stuff."

"Good-bye," I said.

He slid through the bushes and disappeared. I sat where I was, musing, my work interrupted, a mood of bitter disillusionment heavy upon me. So I sat, it may have been for hours.

In the far distance I could hear the faint cry of a bittern in some lonely marsh.

"Now, who the deuce is making that noise?" I muttered. "Some silly fool, I suppose, trying to think he's a waterfowl. Cut it out!"

Long I lay, my dream of the woods shattered, wondering what to do.

Then suddenly there came to my ear the loud sound of voices, human voices, strident and eager, with nothing of the animal growl in them.

"He's in there. I seen him!" I heard some one call.

Rapidly I dived sideways into the underbrush, my animal instinct strong upon me again, growling as I went. Instinctively I knew that it was I that they were after. All the animal joy of being hunted came over me. My union suit stood up on end with mingled fear and rage.

As fast as I could I retreated into the wood. Yet somehow, as I moved, the wood, instead of growing denser, seemed to thin out. I crouched low, still growling and endeavouring to bury myself in the thicket. I was filled with a wild sense of exhilaration such as any lover of the wild life would feel at the knowledge that he is being chased, that some one is after him, that some one is perhaps just a few feet behind him, waiting to stick a pitchfork into him as he runs. There is no ecstasy like this.

Then I realized that my pursuers had closed in on me. I was surrounded on all sides.

The woods had somehow grown thin. They were like the mere shrubbery of a park – it might be of Central Park itself. I could hear among the deeper tones of men the shrill voices of boys. "There he is," one cried, "going through them bushes! Look at him humping himself!" "What is it, what's the sport?" another called. "Some crazy guy loose in the park in his underclothes and the cops after him."

Then they closed in on me. I recognized the blue suits of the police force and their short clubs. In a few minutes I was dragged out of the shrubbery and stood in the open park in my pyjamas, wide awake, shivering in the chilly air of early morning.

Fortunately for me, it was decided at the police-court that sleep-walking is not an offence against the law. I was dismissed with a caution.

My vacation is still before me, and I still propose to spend it naked. But I shall do so at Atlantic City.

❧VII❧

The Cave-Man as He is

I THINK it likely that few people besides myself have ever actually seen and spoken with a "cave-man."

Yet everybody nowadays knows all about the cave-man. The fifteen-cent magazines and the new fiction have made him a familiar figure. A few years ago, it is true, nobody had ever heard of him. But lately, for some reason or other, there has been a run on the cave-man. No up-to-date story is complete without one or two references to him. The hero, when the heroine slights him, is said to "feel for a moment the wild, primordial desire of the cave-man, the longing to seize her, to drag her with him, to carry her away, to make her his." When he takes her in his arms it is recorded that "all the elemental passion of the cave-man surges through him." When he fights, on her behalf, against a dray-man or a gun-man or an ice-man or any other compound that makes up a modern villain, he is said to "feel all the fierce fighting joy of the cave-man." If they kick him in the ribs, he likes it. If they beat him over the head, he never feels it; because he is, for the moment, a cave-man. And the cave-man is, and is known to be, quite above sensation.

The heroine, too, shares the same point of view. "Take me," she murmurs as she falls into the hero's embrace, "be my cave-man." As she says it there is, so the writer assures us, something of the fierce light of the cave-woman in her eyes, the primordial woman to be wooed and won only by force.

So, like everybody else, I had, till I saw him, a great idea of the cave-man. I had a clear mental picture of him – huge, brawny, muscular, a wolfskin thrown about him and a great war-club in his hand. I knew him as without fear with nerves untouched by our effete civilization, fighting, as the beasts fight, to the death, killing without pity and suffering without a moan.

It was a picture that I could not but admire.

I liked, too – I am free to confess it – his peculiar way with women. His system was, as I understood it, to take them by the neck and bring them along with him. That was his fierce, primordial way of "wooing" them. And they liked it. So at least we are informed by a thousand credible authorities. They liked it. And the modern woman, so we are told, would still like it if only one dared to try it on. There's the trouble; if one only *dared!*

I see lots of them – I'll be frank about it – that I should like to grab, to sling over my shoulder and carry away with me; or, what is the same thing, allowing for modern conditions, have an express man carry them. I notice them at Atlantic City, I see them in Fifth Avenue – yes, everywhere.

But would they come? That's the *deuce* of it. Would they come right along, like the cave-woman, merely biting off my ear as they came, or are they degenerate enough to bring an action against me, indicting the express company as a party of the second part?

Doubts such as these prevent me from taking active measures. But they leave me, as they leave many another man, preoccupied and fascinated with the cave-man.

One may imagine, then, my extraordinary interest in him when I actually met him in the flesh. Yet the thing came about quite simply, indeed more by accident than by design, an adventure open to all.

It so happened that I spent my vacation in Kentucky – the region, as everybody knows, of the great caves. They extend – it is a matter of common knowledge – for hundreds of miles; in some places dark and sunless tunnels, the black silence broken only by the dripping of the water from the roof; in other places great vaults like subterranean temples,

69

with vast stone arches sweeping to the dome, and with deep, still water of unfathomed depth as the floor; and here and there again they are lighted from above through rifts in the surface of the earth, and are dry and sand strewn – fit for human habitation.

In such caves as these – so has the obstinate legend run for centuries – there still dwell cave-men, the dwindling remnant of their race. And here it was that I came across him.

I had penetrated into the caves far beyond my guides. I carried a revolver and had with me an electric lantern, but the increasing sunlight in the cave as I went on had rendered the latter needless.

There he sat, a huge figure, clad in a great wolfskin. Besides him lay a great club. Across his knee was a spear round which he was binding sinews that tightened under his muscular hand. His head was bent over his task. His matted hair had fallen over his eyes. He did not see me till I was close beside him on the sanded floor of the cave. I gave a slight cough.

"Excuse me!" I said.

The Cave-man gave a startled jump.

"My goodness," he said, "you startled me!"

I could see that he was quite trembling.

"You came along so suddenly," he said, "it gave me the jumps." Then he muttered, more to himself than to me, "Too much of this darned cave-water! I must quit drinking it."

I sat down near to the Cave-man on a stone, taking care to place my revolver carefully behind it. I don't mind admitting that a loaded revolver, especially as I get older, makes me nervous. I was afraid that he might start fooling with it. One can't be too careful.

As a way of opening conversation I picked up the Cave-man's club.

"Say," I said, "that's a great club you have, eh? By gee! it's heavy!"

"Look out!" said the Cave-man with a certain agitation in his voice as he reached out and took the club from me. "Don't fool with that club! It's loaded! You know you could easily drop the club on your toes, or on mine. A man can't be too careful with a loaded club."

He rose as he said this and carried the club to the other

side of the cave, where he leant it against the wall. Now that he stood up and I could examine him he no longer looked so big. In fact he was not big at all. The effect of size must have come, I think, from the great wolfskin that he wore. I have noticed the same thing in Grand Opera. I noticed, too, for the first time that the cave we were in seemed fitted up, in a rude sort of way, like a dwelling-room.

"This is a nice place you've got," I said.

"Dandy, isn't it?" he said, as he cast his eyes around. "*She* fixed it up. She's got great taste. See that mud sideboard? That's the real thing, A-one mud! None of your cheap rock about that. We fetched that mud for two miles to make that. And look at that wicker bucket. Isn't it great? Hardly leaks at all except through the sides, and perhaps a little through the bottom. *She* wove that. She's a humdinger at weaving."

He was moving about as he spoke, showing me all his little belongings. He reminded me for all the world of a man in a Harlem flat, showing a visitor how convenient it all is. Somehow, too, the Cave-man had lost all appearance of size. He looked, in fact, quite little, and when he had pushed his long hair back from his forehead he seemed to wear that same, worried, apologetic look that we all have. To a higher being, if there is such, our little faces one and all appear, no doubt, pathetic.

I knew that he must be speaking about his wife.

"Where is she?" I asked.

"My wife?" he said. "Oh, she's gone out somewhere through the caves with the kid. You didn't meet our kid as you came along, did you? No? Well, he's the greatest boy you ever saw. He was only two this nineteenth of August. And you should hear him say 'Pop' and 'Mom' just as if he was grown up. He is really, I think, about the brightest boy I've ever known – I mean quite apart from being his father, and speaking of him as if he were anyone else's boy. You didn't meet them?"

"No," I said, "I didn't."

"Oh, well," the Cave-man went on, "there are lots of ways and passages through. I guess they went in another direction. The wife generally likes to take a stroll round in the morning and see some of the neighbours. But, say," he interrupted, "I guess I'm forgetting my manners. Let me get you a drink of cave-water. Here, take it in this stone mug! There you are, say when! Where do we get it? Oh, we find it in parts of the cave where it filters through the soil above. Alcoholic? Oh, yes, about fifteen per cent, I think. Some say it soaks all through the soil of this State. Sit down and be comfortable, and, say, if you hear the woman coming just slip your mug behind that stone out of sight. Do you mind? Now, try one of these elm-root cigars. Oh, pick a good one — there are lots of them!"

We seated ourselves in some comfort on the soft sand, our backs against the boulders, sipping cave-water and smoking elm-root cigars. It seemed altogether as if one were back in civilization, talking to a genial host.

"Yes," said the Cave-man, and he spoke, as it were, in a large and patronizing way. "I generally let my wife trot about as she likes in the daytime. She and the other women nowadays are getting up all these different movements, and the way I look at it is that if it amuses her to run around and talk and attend meetings, why let her do it. Of course," he continued, assuming a look of great firmness, "if I liked to put my foot down —"

"Exactly, exactly," I said. "It's the same way with us!"

"Is it now!" he questioned with interest. "I had imagined that it was all different Outside. You're from the Outside, aren't you? I guessed you must be from the skins you wear."

"Have you never been Outside?" I asked.

"No fear!" said the Cave-man. "Not for mine! Down here in the caves, clean underground and mostly in the dark, it's all right. It's nice and safe." He gave a sort of shudder. "Gee! You fellows out there must have your nerve to go walking around like that on the outside rim of everything, where the stars might fall on you or a thousand things happen to you. But then you Outside Men have got a natural elemental fearlessness about you that we Cave-men have lost. I tell you, I was pretty scared when I looked up and saw you standing there."

"Had you never seen any Outside Men?" I asked.

"Why, yes," he answered, "but never close. The most I've done is to go out to the edges of the cave sometimes and look out and see them, Outside Men and Women, in the distance. But of course, in one way or another, we Cave-men know

72

all about them. And the thing we envy most in you Outside Men is the way you treat your women! By gee! You take no nonsense from them – you fellows are the real primordial, primitive men. We've lost it somehow."

"Why, my dear fellow —" I began.

But the Cave-man, who had sat suddenly upright, interrupted.

"Quick! quick!" he said. "Hide that infernal mug! She's coming. Don't you hear!"

As he spoke I caught the sound of a woman's voice somewhere in the outer passages of the cave.

"Now, Willie," she was saying, speaking evidently to the Cave-child, "you come right along back with me, and if I ever catch you getting in such a mess as that again I'll never take you anywhere, so there!"

Her voice had grown louder. She entered the cave as she spoke – a big-boned woman in a suit of skins leading by the hand a pathetic little mite in a rabbit-skin, with blue eyes and a slobbered face.

But as I was sitting the Cave-woman evidently couldn't see me; for she turned at once to speak to her husband, unconscious of my presence.

"Well, of all the idle creatures!" she exclaimed. "Loafing here in the sand" – she gave a sniff – "and smoking —"

"My dear," began the Cave-man.

"Don't you my-dear me!" she answered. "Look at this place! Nothing tidied up yet and the day half through! Did you put the alligator on to boil?"

"I was just going to say —" began the Cave-man.

"*Going* to say! Yes, I don't doubt you were going to say. You'd go on saying all day if I'd let you. What I'm asking you is, is the alligator on to boil for dinner or is it not — My gracious!" She broke off all of a sudden, as she caught sight of me. "Why didn't you say there was company? Land sakes! And you sit there and never say there was a gentleman here!"

She had hustled across the cave and was busily arranging her hair with a pool of water as a mirror.

"Gracious!" she said, "I'm a perfect fright! You must excuse me," she added, looking round toward me, "for being in this state. I'd just slipped on this old fur blouse and run

73

around to a neighbour's and I'd no idea that he was going to bring in company. Just like him! I'm afraid we've nothing but a plain alligator stoo to offer you, but I'm sure if you'll stay to dinner —"

She was hustling about already, good primitive housewife that she was, making the stone-plates rattle on the mud table.

"Why, really —" I began. But I was interrupted by a sudden exclamation from both the Cave-man and the Cave-woman together:

"Willie! where's Willie!"

"Gracious!" cried the woman. "He's wandered out alone – oh, hurry, look for him! Something might get him! He may have fallen in the water! Oh, hurry!"

They were off in a moment, shouting into the dark passages of the outer cave: "Willie! Willie!" There was agonized anxiety in their voices.

And then in a moment, as it seemed, they were back again, with Willie in their arms, blubbering, his rabbit-skin all wet.

"Goodness gracious!" said the Cave-woman. "He'd fallen right in, the poor little man. Hurry, dear, and get something dry to wrap him in! Goodness, what a fright! Quick, darling, give me something to rub him with."

Anxiously the Cave-parents moved about beside the child, all quarrel vanished.

"But surely," I said, as they calmed down a little, "just there where Willie fell in, beside the passage that I came through, there is only three inches of water."

"So there is," they said, both together, "but just suppose it had been three feet!"

Later on, when Willie was restored, they both renewed their invitation to me to stay to dinner.

"Didn't you say," said the Cave-man, "that you wanted to make some notes on the difference between Cave-people and the people of your world of to-day?"

"I thank you," I answered, "I have already all the notes I want!"

74

❧VIII❧

Ideal Interviews

I WITH A EUROPEAN PRINCE
With any European Prince, travelling in America

ON RECEIVING our card the Prince, to our great surprise and pleasure, sent down a most cordial message that he would be delighted to see us at once. This thrilled us.

"Take us," we said to the elevator boy, "to the apartments of the Prince." We were pleased to see him stagger and lean against his wheel to get his breath back.

In a few moments we found ourselves crossing the threshold of the Prince's apartments. The Prince, who is a charming young man of from twenty-six to twenty-seven, came across the floor to meet us with an extended hand and a simple gesture of welcome. We have seldom seen any-one come across the floor more simply.

The Prince, who is travelling incognito as the Count of Flim Flam, was wearing, when we saw him, the plain morning dress of a gentleman of leisure. We learned that a little earlier he had appeared at breakfast in the costume of a Unitarian clergyman, under the incognito of the Bishop of Bongee; while later on he appeared at lunch, as a delicate compliment to our city, in the costume of a Columbia professor of Yiddish.

The Prince greeted us with the greatest cordiality, seated himself, without the slightest affectation, and motioned to us, with indescribable bonhomie, his permission to remain standing.

75

"Well," said the Prince, "what is it?"

We need hardly say that the Prince, who is a consummate master of ten languages, speaks English quite as fluently as he does Chinese. Indeed, for a moment, we could scarcely tell which he was talking.

"What are your impressions of the United States?" we asked as we took out our notebook.

"I am afraid," answered the Prince, with the delightful smile which is characteristic of him, and which we noticed again and again during the interview, "that I must scarcely tell you that."

We realized immediately that we were in the presence not only of a soldier but of one of the most consummate diplomats of the present day.

"May we ask then," we resumed, correcting our obvious blunder, "what are your impressions, Prince, of the Atlantic Ocean?"

"Ah," said the Prince, with that peculiar thoughtfulness which is so noticeable in him and which we observed not once but several times, "the Atlantic!"

Volumes could not have expressed his thought better.

"Did you," we asked, "see any ice during your passage across?"

"Ah," said the Prince, "ice! Let me think."

We did so.

"Ice," repeated the Prince thoughtfully.

We realized that we were in the presence not only of a soldier, a linguist and a diplomat, but of a trained scientist accustomed to exact research.

"Ice!" repeated the Prince. "Did I see any ice? No."

Nothing could have been more decisive, more final than the clear, simple brevity of the Prince's "No." He had seen no ice. He knew he had seen no ice. He said he had seen no ice. Nothing could have been more straightforward, more direct. We felt assured from that moment that the Prince had not seen any ice.

The exquisite good taste with which the Prince had answered our question served to put us entirely at our ease, and we presently found ourselves chatting with His Highness

76

with the greatest freedom and without the slightest *gêne* or *mauvaise honte*, or, in fact, *malvoisie* of any kind.

We realized, indeed, that we were in the presence not only of a trained soldier, a linguist and a diplomat, but also of a conversationalist of the highest order.

His Highness, who has an exquisite sense of humour – indeed, it broke out again and again during our talk with him – expressed himself as both amused and perplexed over our American money.

"It is very difficult," he said, "with us it is so simple; six and a half gröner are equal to one and a third gross-gröner or the quarter part of our Rigsdaler. Here it is so complicated."

We ventured to show the Prince a fifty-cent piece and to explain its value by putting two quarters beside it.

"I see," said the Prince, whose mathematical ability is quite exceptional, "two twenty-five-cent pieces are equal to one fifty-cent piece. I must try to remember that. Meantime," he added, with a gesture of royal condescension, putting the money in his pocket, "I will keep your coins as instructors" – we murmured our thanks – "and now explain to me, please, your five-dollar gold piece and your ten-dollar eagle."

We felt it proper, however, to shift the subject, and asked the Prince a few questions in regard to his views on American politics. We soon found that His Highness, although this is his first visit to this continent, is a keen student of our institutions and our political life. Indeed, His Altitude showed by his answers to our questions that he is as well informed about our politics as we are ourselves. On being asked what he viewed as the uppermost tendency in our political life of to-day, the Prince replied thoughtfully that he didn't know. To our inquiry as to whether in his opinion democracy was moving forward or backward, the Prince, after a moment of reflection, answered that he had no idea. On our asking which of the generals of our Civil War was regarded in Europe as the greatest strategist, His Highness answered without hesitation, "George Washington."

Before closing our interview the Prince, who, like his illustrious father, is an enthusiastic sportsman, completely

77

turned the tables on us by inquiring eagerly about the prospects for large game in America.

We told him something – as much as we could recollect – of woodchuck hunting in our own section of the country. The Prince was interested at once. His eye lighted up, and the peculiar air of fatigue, or languor, which we had thought to remark on his face during our interview, passed entirely off his features. He asked us a number of questions, quickly and without pausing, with the air, in fact, of a man accustomed to command and not to listen. How was the woodchuck hunted? From horseback or from an elephant? Or from an armoured car, or turret? How many beaters did one use to beat up the woodchuck? What bearers was it necessary to carry with one? How great a danger must one face of having one's beaters killed? What percentage of risk must one be prepared to incur of accidentally shooting one's own beaters? What did a bearer cost? and so on.

All these questions we answered as best we could, the Prince apparently seizing the gist, or essential part of our answer, before we had said it.

In concluding the discussion we ventured to ask His Highness for his autograph. The Prince, who has perhaps a more exquisite sense of humour than any other sovereign of Europe, declared with a laugh that he had no pen. Still roaring over this inimitable drollery, we begged the Prince to honour us by using our own fountain-pen.

"Is there any ink in it?" asked the Prince – which threw us into a renewed paroxysm of laughter.

The Prince took the pen and very kindly autographed for us seven photographs of himself. He offered us more, but we felt that seven was about all we could use. We were still suffocated with laughter over the Prince's wit; His Highness was still signing photographs when an equerry appeared and whispered in the Prince's ear. His Highness, with the consummate tact to be learned only at a court, turned quietly without a word and left the room.

We never, in all our experience, remember seeing a prince – or a mere man for the matter of that – leave a room with greater suavity, discretion, or aplomb. It was a revelation of breeding, of race, of long slavery to caste. And yet, with it all, it seemed to have a touch of finality about it – a hint that the entire proceeding was deliberate, planned, not to be altered by circumstance. He did not come back.

We understand that he appeared later in the morning at a civic reception in the costume of an Alpine Jaeger, and attended the matinée in the dress of a lieutenant of police.

Meantime he has our pen. If he turns up in any costume that we can spot at sight, we shall ask him for it.

II WITH OUR GREATEST ACTOR
That is to say, with Any One of our Sixteen Greatest Actors

It was within the privacy of his own library that we obtained – need we say with infinite difficulty – our interview with the Great Actor. He was sitting in a deep arm-chair, so buried in his own thoughts that he was oblivious of our approach. On his knee before him lay a cabinet photograph of himself. His eyes seemed to be peering into it, as if seeking to fathom its unfathomable mystery. We had time to note that a beautiful carbon photogravure of himself stood on a table at his elbow, while a magnificent half-tone pastel of himself was suspended on a string from the ceiling. It was only when we had seated ourself in a chair and taken out our notebook that the Great Actor looked up.

"An interview?" he said, and we noted with pain the weariness in his tone. "Another interview!"

We bowed.

"Publicity!" he murmured rather to himself than to us. "Publicity! Why must one always be forced into publicity?"

It was not our intention, we explained apologetically, to publish or to print a single word —

"Eh, what?" exclaimed the Great Actor. "Not print it? Not publish it? Then what in —"

Not, we explained, without his consent.

"Ah," he murmured wearily, "my consent. Yes, yes, I must give it. The world demands it. Print, publish anything you like. I am indifferent to praise, careless of fame. Posterity

79

will judge me. But," he added more briskly, "let me see a proof of it in time to make any changes I might care to."

We bowed our assent.

"And now," we began, "may we be permitted to ask a few questions about your art? And first, in which branch of the drama do you consider that your genius chiefly lies, in tragedy or in comedy?"

"In both," said the Great Actor.

"You excel then," we continued, "in neither the one nor the other?"

"Excuse us," we said, "we haven't made our meaning quite clear. What we meant to say is, stated very simply, that you do not consider yourself better in either of them than in the other?"

"Not at all," said the Actor, as he put out his arm with that splendid gesture that we have known and admired for years, at the same time throwing back his leonine head so that his leonine hair fell back from his leonine forehead. "Not at all. I do better in both of them. My genius demands both tragedy and comedy at the same time."

"Ah," we said, as a light broke in upon us, "then that, we presume, is the reason why you are about to appear in to present, I may say, an entirely new Hamlet."

."A new Hamlet!" we exclaimed, fascinated. "A new Ham-Shakespeare?"

The Great Actor frowned.

"I would rather put it," he said, "that Shakespeare is about to appear in me."

"Of course, of course," we murmured, ashamed of our own stupidity.

"I appear," went on the Great Actor, "in *Hamlet*. I expect let! Is such a thing possible?"

"Not at all," he answered, "I excel in each of them."

"Entirely," said the Great Actor, throwing his leonine head forward again. "I have devoted years of study to the part. The whole conception of the part of Hamlet has been wrong."

We sat stunned.

"All actors hitherto," continued the Great Actor, "or rather, I should say, all so-called actors – I mean all those who tried to act before me – have been entirely mistaken in their presentation. They have presented Hamlet as dressed in black velvet."

"Yes, yes," we interjected, "in black velvet, yes!"

"Very good. The thing is absurd," continued the Great Actor, as he reached down two or three heavy volumes from the shelf beside him. "Have you ever studied the Elizabethan era?"

"The which?" we asked modestly.

"The Elizabethan era?"

We were silent.

"Or the pre-Shakespearean tragedy?"

We hung our head.

If you had, you would know that a Hamlet in black velvet is perfectly ridiculous. In Shakespeare's day – as I could prove in a moment if you had the intelligence to understand it – there was no such thing as black velvet. It didn't exist."

"And how then," we asked, intrigued, puzzled and yet delighted, "do *you* present Hamlet?"

"In *brown* velvet," said the Great Actor.

"Great Heavens," we exclaimed, "this is a revolution."

"It is. But that is only one part of my conception. The main thing will be my presentation of what I may call the psychology of Hamlet."

"The psychology!" we said.

"Yes," resumed the Great Actor, "the psychology. To make Hamlet understood, I want to show him as a man bowed down by a great burden. He is overwhelmed with Weltschmerz. He carries in him the whole weight of the Zeitgeist; in fact, everlasting negation lies on him —"

"You mean," we said, trying to speak as cheerfully as we could, "that things are a little bit too much for him."

"His will," went on the Great Actor, disregarding our interruption, "is paralysed. He seeks to move in one direction and is hurled in another. One moment he sinks into the abyss. The next, he rises above the clouds. His feet seek the ground, but find only the air —"

"Wonderful," we said, "but will you not need a good deal of machinery?"

"Machinery!" exclaimed the Great Actor, with a leonine laugh. "The machinery of *thought*, the mechanism of power, of magnetism —"

81

"Ah," we said, "electricity."

"Not at all," said the Great Actor. "You fail to understand. It is all done by my rendering. Take, for example, the famous soliloquy on death. You know it?"

" 'To be or not to be,' " we began.

"Stop," said the Great Actor. "Now observe. It is a soliloquy. Precisely. That is the key to it. It is something that Hamlet *says to himself*. Not a *word of it*, in my interpretation, is actually spoken. All is done in absolute, unbroken silence."

"How on earth," we began, "can you do that?"

"Entirely and solely *with my face*."

Good heavens! Was it possible? We looked again, this time very closely, at the Great Actor's face. We realized with a thrill that it might be done.

"I come before the audience *so*," he went on, "and soliloquize – thus – follow my face, please —"

As the Great Actor spoke, he threw himself into a characteristic pose with folded arms, while gust after gust of emotion, of expression, of alternate hope, doubt and despair, swept – we might say chased themselves across his features.

"Wonderful!" we gasped.

"Shakespeare's lines," said the Great Actor, as his face subsided to its habitual calm, "are not necessary; not, at least, with my acting. The lines, indeed, are mere stage directions, nothing more. I leave them out. This happens again and again in the play. Take, for instance, the familiar scene where Hamlet holds the skull in his hand : Shakespeare here suggests the words 'Alas, poor Yorick! I knew him well —' "

"Yes, yes!" we interrupted, in spite of ourself, " 'a fellow of infinite jest —' "

"Your intonation is awful," said the Actor. "But listen. In my interpretation I use no words at all. I merely carry the skull quietly in my hand, very slowly, across the stage. There I lean against a pillar at the side, with the skull in the palm of my hand, and look at it in silence."

"Wonderful!" we said.

"I then cross over to the right of the stage, very impressively, and seat myself on a plain wooden bench, and remain for some time, looking at the skull."

"Marvellous!"

"I then pass to the back of the stage and lie down on my

stomach, still holding the skull before my eyes. After holding this posture for some time, I crawl slowly forward, portraying by the movement of my legs and stomach the whole sad history of Yorick. Finally I turn my back on the audience, still holding the skull, and convey through the spasmodic movements of my back Hamlet's passionate grief at the loss of his friend."

"Why!" we exclaimed, beside ourself with excitement, "this is not merely a revolution, it is a revelation."

"Call it both," said the Great Actor.

"The meaning of it is," we went on, "that you practically don't need Shakespeare at all."

"Exactly, I do not. I could do better without him. Shakespeare cramps me. What I really mean to convey is not Shakespeare, but something greater, larger – how shall I express it – bigger." The Great Actor paused and we waited, our pencil poised in the air. Then he murmured, as his eyes lifted in an expression of something like rapture. "In fact – ME."

He remained thus, motionless, without moving. We slipped gently to our hands and knees and crawled quietly to the door, and so down the stairs, our notebook in our teeth.

III WITH OUR GREATEST SCIENTIST
As seen in any of our College Laboratories

It was among the retorts and test-tubes of his physical laboratory that we were privileged to interview the Great Scientist. His back was towards us when we entered. With characteristic modesty he kept it so for some time after our entry. Even when he turned round and saw us his face did not react off us as we should have expected.

He seemed to look at us, if such a thing were possible, without seeing us, or, at least, without wishing to see us.

We handed him our card.

He took it, read it, dropped it in a bowlful of sulphuric acid and then, with a quiet gesture of satisfaction, turned again to his work.

We sat for some time behind him. "This, then," we thought to ourselves (we always think to ourselves when we are left alone), "is the man, or rather is the back of the man, who has done more" (here we consulted the notes given us by our editor), "to revolutionize our conception of atomic dynamics than the back of any other man."

Presently the Great Scientist turned towards us with a sigh that seemed to our ears to have a note of weariness in it. Something, we felt, must be making him tired.

"What can I do for you?" he said.

"Professor," we answered, "we have called upon you in response to an overwhelming demand on the part of the public —"

The Great Scientist nodded.

"To learn something of your new researches and discoveries in" (here we consulted a minute card which we carried in our pocket) "in radio-active-emanations which are already becoming" (we consulted our card again) "a household word —"

The Professor raised his hand as if to check us.

"I would rather say," he murmured, "helio-radio-active —"

"So would we," we admitted, "much rather —"

"After all," said the Great Scientist, "helium shares in the most intimate degree the properties of radium. So, too, for the matter of that," he added in afterthought, "do thorium, and borium!"

"Even borium!" we exclaimed, delighted, and writing rapidly in our notebook. Already we saw ourselves writing up as our headline *Borium Shares Properties of Thorium*.

"Just what is it," said the Great Scientist, "that you want to know?"

"Professor," we answered, "what our journal wants is a plain and simple explanation, so clear that even our readers can understand it, of the new scientific discoveries in radium. We understand that you possess, more than any other man, the gift of clear and lucid thought —"

The Professor nodded.

"And that you are able to express yourself with greater simplicity than any two men now lecturing."

The Professor nodded again.

"Now, then," we said, spreading our notes on our knee,

"go at it. Tell us, and, through us, tell a quarter of a million anxious readers just what all these new discoveries are about."

"The whole thing," said the Professor, warming up to his work as he perceived from the motions of our face and ears our intelligent interest, "is simplicity itself. I can give it to you in a word —"

"That's it," we said. "Give it to us that way."

"It amounts, if one may boil it down into a phrase —"

"Boil it, boil it," we interrupted.

"Amounts, if one takes the mere gist of it —"

"Take it," we said, "take it."

"Amounts to the resolution of the ultimate atom."

"Ha!" we exclaimed.

"I must ask you first to clear your mind," the Professor continued, "of all conception of ponderable magnitude."

We nodded. We had already cleared our mind of this.

"In fact," added the Professor, with what we thought a quiet note of warning in his voice, "I need hardly tell you that what we are dealing with must be regarded as altogether ultramicroscopic."

We hastened to assure the Professor that, in accordance with the high standards of honour represented by our journal, we should of course regard anything that he might say as ultramicroscopic and treat it accordingly.

"You say, then," we continued, "that the essence of the problem is the resolution of the atom. Do you think you can give us any idea of what the atom is?"

The Professor looked at us searchingly.

We looked back at him, openly and frankly. The moment was critical for our interview. Could he do it? Were we the kind of person that he could give it to? Could we get it if he did?

"I think I can," he said. "Let us begin with the assumption that the atom is an infinitesimal magnitude. Very good. Let us grant, then, that though it is imponderable and indivisible it must have a spacial content? You grant me this?"

"We do," we said, "we do more than this, we *give* it to you."

"Very well. If spacial, it must have dimension: if dimension – form. Let us assume *ex hypothesi* the form to be that of a spheroid and see where it leads us."

The Professor was now intensely interested. He walked to and fro in his laboratory. His features worked with excitement. We worked ours, too, as sympathetically as we could.

"There is no other possible method in inductive science," he added, "than to embrace some hypothesis, the most attractive that one can find, and remain with it —"

We nodded. Even in our own humble life after our day's work we had found this true.

"Now," said the Professor, planting himself squarely in front of us, "assuming a spherical form, and a spacial content, assuming the dynamic forces that are familiar to us and assuming – the thing is bold, I admit —"

We looked as bold as we could.

"Assuming that the *ions*, or *nuclei* of the atom – I know no better word —"

"Neither do we," we said.

"That the nuclei move under the energy of such forces, what have we got?"

"Ha!" we said.

"What have we got? Why, the simplest matter conceivable. The forces inside our atom – itself, mind you, the function of a circle – mark that –"

We did.

"Becomes merely a function of π!"

The Great Scientist paused with a laugh of triumph.

"A function of π!" we repeated in delight.

"Precisely. Our conception of ultimate matter is reduced to that of an oblate spheroid described by the revolution of an ellipse on its own minor axis!"

"Good heavens!" we said. "Merely that."

"Nothing else. And in that case any further calculation becomes a mere matter of the extraction of a root."

"How simple," we murmured.

"Is it not," said the Professor. "In fact, I am accustomed, in talking to my class, to give them a very clear idea, by simply taking as our root F – F being any finite constant —"

He looked at us sharply. We nodded.

"And raising F to the log of infinity. I find they apprehend it very readily."

"Do they?" we murmured. Ourselves we felt as if the Log of Infinity carried us to ground higher than what we commonly care to tread on.

"Of course," said the Professor, "the Log of Infinity is an Unknown."

"Of course," we said very gravely. We felt ourselves here in the presence of something that demanded our reverence.

"But still," continued the Professor almost jauntily, "we can handle the Unknown just as easily as anything else."

This puzzled us. We kept silent. We thought it wiser to move on to more general ground. In any case, our notes were now nearly complete.

"These discoveries, then," we said, "are absolutely revolutionary."

"They are," said the Professor.

"You have now, as we understand, got the atom – how shall we put it? – got it where you want it."

"Not exactly," said the Professor with a sad smile.

"What do you mean?" we asked.

"Unfortunately our analysis, perfect though it is, stops short. We have no synthesis."

The Professor spoke as in deep sorrow.

"No synthesis," we moaned. We felt it was a cruel blow. But in any case our notes were now elaborate enough. We felt that our readers could do without a synthesis. We rose to go.

"Synthetic dynamics," said the Professor, taking us by the coat, "is only beginning —"

"In that case —" we murmured, disengaging his hand.

"But, wait, wait," he pleaded "wait for another fifty years —"

"We will," we said very earnestly. "But meantime as our paper goes to press this afternoon we must go now. In fifty years we will come back."

"Oh, I see, I see," said the Professor, "you are writing all this for a newspaper. I see."

"Yes," we said, "we mentioned that at the beginning."

"Ah," said the Professor, "did you? Very possibly. Yes."

"We propose," we said, "to feature the article for next Saturday."

"Will it be long?" he asked.

"About two columns," we answered.

"And how much," said the Professor in a hesitating way, "do I have to pay you to put it in?"

"How much which?" we asked.

"How much do I have to pay?"

"Why, Professor —" we began quickly. Then we checked ourselves. After all was it right to undeceive him, this quiet, absorbed man of science with his ideals, his atoms and his emanations. No, a hundred times no. Let him pay a hundred times.

"It will cost you," we said very firmly, "ten dollars."

The Professor began groping among his apparatus. We knew that he was looking for his purse.

"We should like also very much," we said, "to insert your picture along with the article —"

"Would that cost much?" he asked.

"No, that is only five dollars."

The Professor had meantime found his purse.

"Would it be all right," he began, "that is, would you mind if I pay you the money now? I am apt to forget."

"Quite all right," we answered. We said good-bye very gently and passed out. We felt somehow as if we had touched a higher life. "Such," we murmured, as we looked about the ancient campus, "are the men of science: are there, perhaps, any others of them round this morning that we might interview?"

IV WITH OUR TYPICAL NOVELISTS
Edwin and Ethelinda Afterthought—Husband and Wife—In their Delightful Home Life.

It was at their beautiful country place on the Woonagan-sett that we had the pleasure of interviewing the Afterthoughts. At their own cordial invitation, we had walked over from the nearest railway station, a distance of some fourteen miles. Indeed, as soon as they heard of our intention they invited us to walk. "We are so sorry not to bring you in the motor," they wrote, "but the roads are so frightfully dusty that we might get dust on our chauffeur." This little touch of thoughtfulness is the keynote of their character.

The house itself is a delightful old mansion giving on a wide garden, which gives in turn on a broad terrace giving on the river.

The Eminent Novelist met us at the gate. We had expected to find the author of *Angela Rivers* and *The Garden of Desire* a pale aesthetic type (we have a way of expecting the wrong thing in our interviews). We could not resist a shock of surprise (indeed we seldom do) at finding him a burly out-of-door man weighting, as he himself told us, a hundred stone in his stockinged feet (we think he said stone).

He shook hands cordially.

"Come and see my pigs," he said.

"We wanted to ask you," we began, as we went down the walk, "something about your books."

"Let's look at the pigs first," he said. "Are you anything of a pig man?"

We are always anxious in our interviews to be all things to all men. But we were compelled to admit that we were not much of a pig man.

"Ah," said the Great Novelist, "perhaps you are more of a dog man?"

"Not altogether a dog man," we answered.

"Anything of a bee man?" he asked.

"Something," we said (we were once stung by a bee).

"Ah," he said, "you shall have a go at the beehives, then, right away?"

We assured him that we were willing to postpone a go at the beehives till later.

"Come along, then, to the styes," said the Great Novelist, and he added, "Perhaps you're not much of a breeder."

We blushed. We thought of the five little faces around the table for which we provide food by writing our interviews.

"No," we said, "we were not much of a breeder."

"Now then," said the Great Novelist as we reached our goal, "how do you like this stye?"

"Very much indeed," we said.

"I've put in a new tile draining – my own plan. You notice how sweet it keeps the stye."

We had not noticed this.

"I am afraid," said the Novelist, "that the pigs are all asleep inside."

We begged him on no account to waken them. He offered to open the little door at the side and let us crawl in. We insisted that we could not think of intruding.

"What we would like," we said, "is to hear something of your methods of work in novel writing." We said this with very peculiar conviction. Quite apart from the immediate purposes of our interview, we have always been most anxious to know by what process novels are written. If we could get to know this, we would write one ourselves.

"Come and see my bulls first," said the Novelist. "I've got a couple of young bulls here in the paddock that will interest you."

We felt sure that they would.

He led us to a little green fence. Inside it were two ferocious looking animals, eating grain. They rolled their eyes upwards at us as they ate.

"How do those strike you?" he asked.

We assured him that they struck us as our beau ideal of bulls.

"Like to walk in beside them?" said the Novelist, opening a little gate.

We drew back. Was it fair to disturb these bulls?

The Great Novelist noticed our hesitation.

"Don't be afraid," he said. "They're not likely to harm you. I send my hired man right in beside them every morning, without the slightest hesitation."

We looked at the Eminent Novelist with admiration. We realized that like so many of our writers, actors, and even our thinkers, of to-day, he was an open-air man in every sense of the word.

But we shook our heads.

Bulls, we explained, were not a department of research for which we were equipped. What we wanted, we said, was to learn something of his methods of work.

"My methods of work?" he answered, as we turned up the path again. "Well, really, I hardly know that I have any."

"What is your plan or method," we asked, getting out our

notebook and pencil, "of laying the beginning of a new novel?"

"My usual plan," said the Novelist, "is to come out here and sit in the stye till I get my characters."

"Does it take long?" we questioned.

"Not very. I generally find that a quiet half-hour spent among the hogs will give me at least my leading character."

"And what do you do next?"

"Oh, after that I generally light a pipe and go and sit among the beehives looking for an incident."

"Do you get it?" we asked.

"Invariably. After that I make a few notes, then go off for a ten mile tramp with my esquimaux dogs, and get back in time to have a go through the cattle sheds and take a romp with the young bulls."

We sighed. We couldn't help it. Novel writing seemed further away than ever.

"Have you also a goat on the premises?" we asked.

"Oh, certainly. A ripping old fellow – come along and see him."

We shook our heads. No doubt our disappointment showed in our face. It often does. We felt that it was altogether right and wholesome that our great novels of to-day should be written in this fashion with the help of goats, dogs, hogs and young bulls. But we felt, too, that it was not for us.

We permitted ourselves one further question.

"At what time," we said, "do you rise in the morning?"

"Oh anywhere between four and five," said the Novelist.

"Ah, and do you generally take a cold dip as soon as you are up – even in winter?"

"I do."

"You prefer, no doubt," we said, with a dejection that we could not conceal, "to have water with a good coat of ice over it?"

"Oh, certainly!"

We said no more. We have long understood the reasons for our own failure in life, but it was painful to receive a renewed corroboration of it. This ice question has stood in our way for forty-seven years.

The Great Novelist seemed to note our dejection.

"Come to the house," he said, "my wife will give you a cup of tea."

In a few moments we had forgotten all our troubles in the presence of one of the most charming chatelaines it has been our lot to meet.

We sat on a low stool immediately beside Ethelinda Afterthought, who presided in her own gracious fashion over the tea-urn.

"So you want to know something of my methods of work?" she said, as she poured hot tea over our leg.

"We do," we answered, taking out our little book and re-covering something of our enthusiasm. We do not mind hot tea being poured over us if people treat us as a human being.

"Can you indicate," we continued, "what method you follow in beginning one of your novels?"

"I always begin," said Ethelinda Afterthought, "with a study."

"A study?" we queried.

"Yes. I mean a study of actual facts. Take, for example, my *Leaves from the Life of a Steam Laundrywoman* – more tea?"

"No, no," we said.

"Well, to make that book I first worked two years in a laundry."

"Two years!" we exclaimed. "And why?"

"To get the atmosphere."

"The steam?" we questioned.

"Oh, no," said Mrs. Afterthought, "I did that separately. I took a course in steam at a technical school."

"Is it possible?" we said, our heart beginning to sing again. "Was all that necessary?"

"I don't see how one could do it otherwise. The story opens, as no doubt you remember – tea? – in the boiler room of the laundry."

"Yes," we said, moving our leg — "no, thank you."

"So you see the only possible *point d'appui* was to begin with a description of the inside of the boiler."

We nodded.

"A masterly thing," we said.

"My wife," interrupted the Great Novelist, who was sitting with the head of a huge Danish hound in his lap, sharing his

92

buttered toast with the dog while he adjusted a set of trout flies, "is a great worker."

"Do you always work on that method?" we asked.

"Always," she answered. "For *Frederica of the Factory* I spent six months in a knitting mill. For *Marguerite of the Mud Flats* I made special studies for months and months."

"Of what sort?" we asked.

"In mud. Learning to model it. You see for a story of that sort the first thing needed is a thorough knowledge of mud — all kinds of it."

"And what are you doing next?" we inquired.

"My next book," said the Lady Novelist, "is to be a study — tea? — of the pickle industry — perfectly new ground."

"A fascinating field," we murmured.

"And quite new. Several of our writers have done the slaughter-house, and in England a good deal has been done in jam. But so far no one has done pickles. I should like, if I could," added Ethelinda Afterthought, with the graceful modesty that is characteristic of her, "to make it the first of a series of pickle novels, showing, don't you know, the whole pickle district, and perhaps following a family of pickle workers for four or five generations."

"Four or five!" we said enthusiastically. "Make it ten! And have you any plan for work beyond that?"

"Oh, yes indeed," laughed the Lady Novelist. "I am always planning ahead. What I want to do after that is a study of the inside of a penitentiary."

"Of the *inside*?" we said, with a shudder.

"Yes. To do it, of course, I shall go to jail for two or three years!"

"But how can you get in?" we asked, thrilled at the quiet determination of the frail woman before us.

"I shall demand it as a right," she answered quietly. "I shall go to the authorities, at the head of a band of enthusiastic women, and demand that I shall be sent to jail. Surely after the work I have done, that much is coming to me."

"It certainly is," we said warmly.

We rose to go.

Both the novelists shook hands with us with great cordiality. Mr. Afterthought walked as far as the front door with us and showed us a short cut past the beehives that could take us directly through the bull pasture to the main road.

We walked away in the gathering darkness of evening very quietly. We made up our mind as we went that novel writing is not for us. We must reach the penitentiary in some other way.

But we thought it well to set down our interview as a guide to others.

❈ IX ❈

The New Education

So you're going back to college in a fortnight," I said to the Bright Young Thing on the veranda of the summer hotel. "Aren't you sorry?"

"In a way I am," she said, "but in another sense I'm glad to go back. One can't loaf all the time."

She looked up from her rocking-chair over her Red Cross knitting with great earnestness.

How full of purpose these modern students are, I thought to myself. In my time we used to go back to college as to a treadmill.

"I know that," I said, "but what I mean is that college, after all, is a pretty hard grind. Things like mathematics and Greek are no joke, are they? In my day, as I remember it, we used to think spherical trigonometry about the hardest stuff of the lot."

She looked dubious.

"I didn't *elect* mathematics," she said.

"Oh," I said, "I see. So you don't have to take it. And what *have* you elected?"

"For this coming half semester – that's six weeks, you know – I've elected Social Endeavour."

"Ah," I said, "that's since my day, what is it?"

"Oh, it's *awfully* interesting. It's the study of conditions."

"What kind of conditions?" I asked.

"All conditions. Perhaps I can't explain it properly. But I have the prospectus of it indoors if you'd like to see it. We take up Society."

"And what do you do with it?"

"Analyse it," she said.

"But it must mean reading a tremendous lot of books."

"No," she answered. "We don't use books in this course. It's all Laboratory Work."

"Now I *am* mystified," I said. "What *do* you mean by Laboratory Work?"

"Well," answered the girl student with a thoughtful look upon her face, "you see, we are supposed to break society up into its elements."

"In six weeks?"

"Some of the girls do it in six weeks. Some put in a whole semester and take twelve weeks at it."

"So as to break up pretty thoroughly?" I said.

"Yes," she assented. "But most of the girls think six weeks is enough."

"That ought to pulverize it pretty completely. But how do you go at it?"

"Well," the girl said, "it's all done with Laboratory Work. We take, for instance, department stores. I think that is the first thing we do, we take up the department store."

"And what do you do with it?"

"We study it as a Social Germ."

"Ah," I said, "as a Social Germ."

"Yes," said the girl, delighted to see that I was beginning to understand, "as a Germ. All the work is done in the concrete. The class goes down with the professor to the department store itself —"

"And then —"

"Then they walk all through it, observing."

"But have none of them ever been in a departmental store before?"

"Oh, of course, but, you see, we go as Observers."

"Ah, now, I understand. You mean you don't buy anything and so you are able to watch everything?"

"No," she said, "it's not that. We do buy things. That's part of it. Most of the girls like to buy little knick-knacks, and anyway it gives them a good chance to do their shopping while they're there. But while they *are* there they are observing. Then afterwards they make charts."

"Charts of what?" I asked.

"Charts of the employés; they're used to show the brain movement involved."

"Do you find much?"

"Well," she said hesitatingly, "the idea is to reduce all the employés to a Curve."

"To a Curve?" I exclaimed, "an In or an Out."

"No, no, not exactly that. Didn't you use Curves when you were at college?"

"Never," I said.

"Oh, well, nowadays nearly everything, you know, is done into a Curve. We put them on the board."

"And what is this particular Curve of the employé used for?" I asked.

"Why," said the student, "the idea is that from the Curve we can get the Norm of the employé."

"Get his Norm?" I asked.

"Yes, get the Norm. That stands for the Root Form of the employé as a social factor."

"And what can you do with that?"

"Oh, when we have that we can tell what the employé would do under any and every circumstance. At least that's the idea – though I'm really only quoting," she added, breaking off in a diffident way, "from what Miss Thinker, the professor of Social Endeavour, says. She's really fine. She's making a general chart of the female employés of one of the biggest stores to show what percentage in case of fire would jump out of the window and what percentage would run to the fire escape."

"It's a wonderful course," I said. "We had nothing like it when I went to college. And does it only take in departmental stores?"

"No," said the girl, "the laboratory work includes for this semester ice-cream parlours as well."

"What do you do with *them*?"

"We take them up as Social Cells, Nuclei, I think the professor calls them."

"And how do you go at them?" I asked.

"Why, the girls go to them in little laboratory groups and study them."

"They eat ice-cream in them?"

"They *have* to," she said, "to make it concrete. But while they are doing it they are considering the ice-cream parlour merely as a section of social protoplasm."

"Does the professor go?" I asked.

"Oh, yes, she heads each group. Professor Thinker never spares herself from work."

"Dear me," I said, "you must be kept very busy. And is Social Endeavour all that you are going to do?"

"No," she answered, "I'm electing a half-course in Nature Work as well."

"Nature Work? Well! Well! That, I suppose, means cramming up a lot of biology and zoology, does it not?"

"No," said the girl, "it's not exactly done with *books*. I believe it is all done by Field Work."

"Field Work?"

"Yes. Field Work four times a week and an Excursion every Saturday."

"And what do you do in the Field Work?"

"The girls," she answered, "go out in groups anywhere out of doors, and make a Nature Study of anything they see."

"How do they do that?" I asked.

"Why, they look at it. Suppose, for example, they come to a stream or a pond or anything —"

"Yes —"

"Well, they *look* at it."

"Had they never done that before?" I asked.

"Ah, but they look at it as a Nature Unit. Each girl must take forty units in the course. I think we only do one unit each day we go out."

"It must," I said, "be pretty fatiguing work, and what about the Excursion?"

"That's every Saturday. We go out with Miss Stalk, the professor of Ambulation."

"And where do you go?"

"Oh, anywhere. One day we go perhaps for a trip on a steamer and another Saturday somewhere in motors, and so on."

"Doing what?" I asked.

"Field Work. The aim of the course – I'm afraid I'm quoting Miss Stalk but I don't mind, she's really fine – is to break nature into its elements —"

"I see —"

"So as to view it as the external structure of Society and make deductions from it."

"Have you made any?" I asked.

"Oh, no" – she laughed – "I'm only starting the work this term. But, of course, I shall have to. Each girl makes at least one deduction at the end of the course. Some of the seniors make two or three. But you have to make *one*."

"It's a great course," I said. "No wonder you are going to be busy; and, as you say, how much better than loafing round here doing nothing."

"Isn't it?" said the girl student with enthusiasm in her eyes. "It gives one such a sense of purpose, such a feeling of doing something."

"It must," I answered.

"Oh, goodness," she exclaimed, "there's the lunch bell. I must skip and get ready."

She was just vanishing from my side when the Burly Male Student, who was also staying in the hotel, came puffing up after his five-mile run. He was getting himself into trim for enlistment, so he told me. He noted the retreating form of the college girl as he sat down.

"I've just been talking to her," I said, "about her college work. She seems to be studying a queer lot of stuff – Social Endeavour and all that!"

"Awful piffle," said the young man. "But the girls naturally run to all that sort of rot, you know."

"Now, your work," I went on, "is no doubt very different. I mean what you were taking before the war came along. I suppose you fellows have an awful dose of mathematics and philology and so on just as I did in my college days?"

Something like a blush came across the face of the handsome youth.

"Well, no," he said, "I didn't co-opt mathematics. At our college, you know, we co-opt two majors and two minors."

"I see," I said, "and what were you co-opting?"

"I co-opted Turkish, Music, and Religion," he answered.

"Oh, yes," I said with a sort of reverential respect, "fitting yourself for a position of choir-master in a Turkish cathedral, no doubt."

"No, no," he said, "I'm going into insurance; but, you see, those subjects fitted in better than anything else."

"Fitted in?"

"Yes. Turkish comes at nine, music at ten and religion at eleven. So they make a good combination; they leave a man free to —"

"To develop his mind," I said. "We used to find in my college days that lectures interfered with it badly. But now, Turkish, that must be an interesting language, eh?"

"Search me!" said the student. "All you have to do is answer the roll and go out. Forty roll-calls give you one Turkish unit – but, say, I must get on, I've got to change. So long."

I could not help reflecting, as the young man left me, on the great changes that have come over our college education. It was a relief to me later in the day to talk with a quiet, sombre man, himself a graduate student in philosophy, on this topic. He agreed with me that the old strenuous studies seem to be very largely abandoned.

I looked at the sombre man with respect.

"Now your work," I said, "is very different from what these young people are doing – hard, solid, definite effort. What a relief it must be to you to get a brief vacation up here. I couldn't help thinking to-day, as I watched you moving round doing nothing, how fine it must feel for you to come up here after your hard work and put in a month of out-and-out loafing."

"Loafing!" he said indignantly. "I'm not loafing. I'm putting in a half summer course in Introspection. That's why I'm here. I get credit for two majors for my time here."

"Ah," I said, as gently as I could, "you get credit here."

He left me. I am still pondering over our new education. Meantime I think I shall enter my little boy's name on the books of Tuskegee College where the education is still old-fashioned.

The Errors of Santa Claus

IT WAS Christmas Eve

The Browns, who lived in the adjoining house, had been dining with the Joneses.

Brown and Jones were sitting over wine and walnuts at the table. The others had gone upstairs.

"What are you giving to your boy for Christmas?" asked Brown.

"A train," said Jones, "new kind of thing – automatic."

"Let's have a look at it," said Brown.

Jones fetched a parcel from the sideboard and began unwrapping it.

"Ingenious thing, isn't it?" he said. "Goes on its own rails. Queer how kids love to play with trains, isn't it?"

"Yes," assented Brown. "How are the rails fixed?"

"Wait, I'll show you," said Jones. "Just help me to shove these dinner things aside and roll back the cloth. There! See! You lay the rails like that and fasten them at the ends, so —"

"Oh, yes, I catch on, makes a grade, doesn't it? Just the thing to amuse a child, isn't it? I got Willy a toy aeroplane."

"I know, they're great. I got Edwin one on his birthday. But I thought I'd get him a train this time. I told him Santa Claus was going to bring him something altogether new this time. Edwin, of course, believes in Santa Claus absolutely. Say, look at this locomotive, would you? It has a spring coiled up inside the fire box."

"Wind her up," said Brown with great interest. "Let's see her go."

"All right," said Jones. "Just pile up two or three plates or something to lean the end of the rails on. There, notice the way it buzzes before it starts. Isn't that a great thing for a kid, eh?"

"Yes," said Brown. "And say, see this little string to pull the whistle! By Gad, it toots, eh? Just like real?"

"Now then, Brown," Jones went on, "you hitch on those cars and I'll start her. I'll be engineer, eh!"

Half an hour later Brown and Jones were still playing trains on the dining-room table.

But their wives upstairs in the drawing-room hardly noticed their absence. They were too much interested.

"Oh, I think it's perfectly sweet," said Mrs. Brown. "Just the loveliest doll I've seen in years. I must get one like it for Ulvina. Won't Clarisse be perfectly enchanted?"

"Yes," answered Mrs. Jones, "and then she'll have all the fun of arranging the dresses. Children love that so much. Look, there are three little dresses with the doll, aren't they cute? All cut out and ready to stitch together."

"Oh, how perfectly lovely!" exclaimed Mrs. Brown. "I think the mauve one would suit the doll best, don't you, with such golden hair? Only don't you think it would make it much nicer to turn back the collar, so, and to put a little band – so?"

"*What* a good idea!" said Mrs. Jones. "Do let's try it. Just wait, I'll get a needle in a minute. I'll tell Clarisse that Santa Claus sewed it himself. The child believes in Santa Claus absolutely."

And half an hour later Mrs. Jones and Mrs. Brown were so busy stitching dolls' clothes that they could not hear the roaring of the little train up and down the dining table, and had no idea what the four children were doing.

Nor did the children miss their mothers.

"Dandy, aren't they?" Edwin Jones was saying to little Willie Brown, as they sat in Edwin's bedroom. "A hundred in a box, with cork tips, and see, an amber mouthpiece that fits into a little case at the side. Good present for Dad, eh?"

"Fine!" said Willie appreciativly. "I'm giving Father cigars."

"I know, I thought of cigars too. Men always like cigars and cigarettes. You can't go wrong on them. Say, would you like to try one or two of these cigarettes? We can take them from the bottom. You'll like them, they're Russian – away ahead of Egyptian."

"Thanks," answered Willie. "I'd like one immensely. I only started smoking last spring – on my twelfth birthday. I think a feller's a fool to begin smoking cigarettes too soon, don't you? It stunts him. I waited till I was twelve."

"Me too," said Edwin, as they lighted their cigarettes. "In fact, I wouldn't buy them now if it weren't for Dad. I simply *had* to give him something from Santa Claus. He believes in Santa Claus absolutely, you know."

And, while this was going on, Clarisse was showing little Ulvina the absolutely lovely little bridge set that she got for her mother.

"Aren't these markers perfectly charming?" said Ulvina. "And don't you love this little Dutch design – or is it Flemish, darling?"

"Dutch," said Clarisse. "Isn't it quaint? And aren't these the dearest little things, for putting the money in when you play. I needn't have got them with it – they'd have sold the rest separately – but I think it's too utterly slow playing without money, don't you?"

"Oh, abominable," shuddered Ulvina. "But your mamma never plays for money, does she?"

"Mamma! Oh, gracious, no. Mamma's far too slow for that. But I shall tell her that Santa Claus insisted on putting in the little money boxes."

"I suppose she believes in Santa Claus, just as my mamma does."

"Oh, absolutely," said Clarisse, and added, "What if we play a little game! With a double dummy, the French way, or Norwegian Skat, if you like. That only needs two."

"All right," agreed Ulvina, and in a few minutes they were deep in a game of cards with a little pile of pocket money beside them.

About half an hour later, all the members of the two families were again in the drawing-room. But of course nobody said anything about the presents. In any case they were all too busy looking at the beautiful big Bible, with maps in it, that the Joneses had brought to give to Grandfather. They all agreed that, with the help of it, Grandfather could hunt up any place in Palestine in a moment, day or night.

But upstairs, away upstairs in a sitting-room of his own Grandfather Jones was looking with an affectionate eye at the presents that stood beside him. There was a beautiful whisky decanter, with silver filigree outside (and whiskey inside) for Jones, and for the little boy a big nickel-plated Jew's harp.

Later on, far in the night, the person, or the influence, or whatever it is called Santa Claus, took all the presents and placed them in the people's stockings.

And, being blind as he always has been, he gave the wrong things to the wrong people – in fact, he gave them just as indicated above.

But the next day, in the course of Christmas morning, the situation straightened itself out, just as it always does.

Indeed, by ten o'clock, Brown and Jones were playing with the train, and Mrs. Brown and Mrs. Jones were making dolls' clothes, and the boys were smoking cigarettes, and Clarisse and Ulvina were playing cards for their pocket-money.

And upstairs – away up – Grandfather was drinking whisky and playing the Jew's harp.

And so Christmas, just as it always does, turned out all right after all.

❖ XI ❖

Lost in New York

A VISITOR'S SOLILOQUY

WELL! WELL!

Whatever has been happening to this place, to New York? Changed? Changed since I was here in '86? Well, I should say so.

The hack-driver of the old days that I used to find waiting for me at the station curb, with that impossible horse of his – the hack-driver with his bulbous red face, and the nice smell of rye whisky all 'round him for yards – gone, so it seems, for ever.

And in place of him this – what is it they call it? – taxi, with a clean-shaven cut-throat steering it. "Get in," he says, Just that. He doesn't offer to help me or lift my satchel. All right, young man, I'm crawling in.

That's the machine that marks it, eh? I suppose they have them rigged up so they can punch up anything they like. I thought so – he hits it up to fifty cents before we start. But I saw him do it. Well, I can stand for it this time. I'll not be caught in one of these again.

The hotel? All right, I'm getting out. My hotel? But what is it they have done to it? They must have added ten stories to it. It reaches to the sky. But I'll not try to look to the top of it. Not with this satchel in my hand: no, sir! I'll wait till I'm safe inside. In there I'll feel all right. They'll know me in there. They'll remember right away my visit in the fall of '86. They won't easily have forgotten that big dinner I gave — nine people at a dollar fifty a plate, with the cigars extra. The clerk will remember *me*, all right.

Know me? Not they. The *clerk* know me! How could he? For it seems now there isn't any clerk, or not as there used to be. They have subdivided him somehow into five or six. There is a man behind a desk, a majestic sort of man, waving his hand. It would be sheer madness to claim acquaintance with him. There is another with a great book, adjusting cards in it; and another, behind glass labelled "Cashier," and busy as a bank; there are two with mail and telegrams. They are all too busy to know me.

Shall I sneak up near to them, keeping my satchel in my hand? I wonder, do they *see* me? *Can* they see me, a mere thing like me? I am within ten feet of them, but I am certain that they cannot see me. I am, and I feel it, absolutely invisible.

Ha! One has seen me. He turns to me, or rather he rounds upon me, with the words "Well, sir?" That, and nothing else, sharp and hard. There is none of the ancient kindly pretence of knowing my name, no reaching out a welcome hand and calling me Mr. Er – Er – till he has read my name upside down while I am writing it and can address me as a familiar friend. No friendly questioning about the crops in my part of the country. The crops, forsooth! What do these young men know about crops?

A room? Had I any reservation? Any which? Any reservation. Oh, I see, had I written down from home to say that I was coming? No, I had not because the truth is I came at very short notice. I didn't know till a week before that my brother-in-law — He is not listening. He has moved away. I will stand and wait till he comes back. I am intruding here; I had no right to disturb these people like this.

Oh, I can have a room at eleven o'clock. When it is which? – is vacated. Oh, yes, I see, when the man in it gets up and goes away. I didn't for the minute catch on to what the word — He has stopped listening.

Never mind, I can wait. From eight to eleven is only three hours, anyway. I will move about here and look at things. If I keep moving they will notice me less. Ha! books and newspapers and magazines – what a stack of them! Like a regular book-store. I will stand here and take a look at some of them. Eh! what's that? Did I want to *buy* anything? Well, no, I hadn't exactly – I was just – Oh, I see, they're on *sale*. All right, yes, give me this one – fifty cents – all right – and this and these others. That's all right, miss, I'm not stingy. They always say of me up in our town that when I — She has stopped listening.

Never mind. I will walk up and down again with the magazines under my arm. That will make people think I live here. Better still if I could put the magazines in my satchel. But how? There is no way to set it down and undo the straps. I wonder if I could dare put it for a minute on that table, the polished one —? Or no, they wouldn't likely allow a man to put a bag *there*.

Well, I can wait. Anyway, it's eight o'clock and soon, surely, breakfast will be ready. As soon as I hear the gong I can go in there. I wonder if I could find out first where the dining-room is. It used always to be marked across the door, but I don't seem to see it. Darn it, I'll ask that man in uniform. If I'm here prepared to spend my good money to get breakfast I guess I'm not scared to ask a simple question of a man in uniform. Or no, I'll not ask *him*. I'll try this one – or no, he's busy. I'll ask this other boy. Say, would you mind, if you please, telling me, please, which way the dining-room – Eh, what? Do I want which? The grill room or the palm room? Why, I tell you, young man, I just wanted to get some breakfast if it's – what? Do I want what? I didn't quite get that – *à la carte*? No, thanks – and, what's that? table de what? in the palm room? No, I just wanted – but it doesn't matter. I'll wait 'round here and look about till I hear the gong. Don't worry about me.

What's that? What's that boy shouting out – that boy with the tray? A call for Mr. Something or Other – say, must be something happened pretty serious! A call for Mr. – why, that's for me! Hullo! *Here I am! Here, it's Me! Here I am* – wanted at the desk? all right, I'm coming, I'm hurrying. I guess something's wrong at home, eh! *Here I am.* That's my name. I'm ready.

Oh, a room. You've got a room for me. All right. The fifteenth floor! Good heavens! Away up there! Never mind,

I'll take it. Can't give me a bath? That's all right. I had one.

Elevator over this way? All right, I'll come along. Thanks, I can carry it. But I don't see any elevator? Oh, this door in the wall? Well! I'm hanged. This the elevator! It certainly has changed. The elevator that I remember had a rope in the middle of it, and you pulled the rope up as you went, wheezing and clanking all the way to the fifth floor. But this looks a queer sort of machine. How do you do – Oh, I beg your pardon. I was in the road of the door, I guess. Excuse me, I'm afraid I got in the way of your elbow. It's all right, you didn't hurt – or, not bad.

Gee whiz! It goes fast. Are you sure you can stop it? Better be careful, young man. There was an elevator once in our town that – fifteenth floor? All right.

This room, eh! Great Scott, it's high up. Say, better not go too near that window, boy. That would be a hell of a drop if a feller fell out. You needn't wait. Oh, I see. I beg your pardon. I suppose a quarter is enough, eh?"

Well, it's a relief to be alone. But say, this is high up! And what a noise! What is it they're doing out there, away out in the air, with all that clatter – building a steel building, I guess. Well, those fellers have their nerve, all right. I'll sit further back from the window.

It's lonely up here. In the old days I could have rung a bell and had a drink sent up to the room; but away up here on the fifteenth floor! Oh, no, they'd never send a drink clean up to the fifteenth floor. Of course, in the old days, I could have put on my canvas slippers and walked down to the bar and had a drink and talked to the bar-tender.

But of course they wouldn't have a bar in a place like this. I'd like to go down and see, but I don't know that I'd care to ask, anyway. No, I guess I'll just sit and wait. Some one will come for me, I guess, after a while.

If I were back right now in our town, I could walk into Ed Clancey's restaurant and have ham and eggs, or steak and eggs, or anything, for thirty-five cents.

Our town up home is a peach of a little town, anyway.

Say, I just feel as if I'd like to take my satchel and jump clean out of that window. It would be a good rebuke to them.

But, pshaw! what would *they* care?

❧ XII ❧

This Strenuous Age

SOMETHING is happening, I regret to find, to the world in which we used to live. The poor old thing is being "speeded up." There is "efficiency" in the air. Offices open at eight o'clock. Millionaires lunch on a baked apple. Bankers eat practically nothing. A college president has declared that there are more foot pounds of energy in a glass of peptonized milk than in — something else, I forget what. All this is very fine. Yet somehow I feel out of it.

My friends are failing me. They won't sit up after midnight. They have taken to sleeping out of doors, on porches and pergolas. Some, I understand, merely roost on plain wooden bars. They rise early. They take deep breathing. They bathe in ice water. They are no good.

This change, I am sure, is excellent. It is, I am certain, just as it ought to be. I am merely saying, quietly and humbly, that I am not in it. I am being left behind. Take, for example, the case of alcohol. That, at least, is what it is called now. There were days when we called it Bourbon whisky and Tom Gin, and when the very name of it breathed romance. That time is past.

The poor stuff is now called alcohol, and none so low that he has a good word for it. Quite right, I am certain. I don't defend it. Alcohol, they are saying to-day, if taken in sufficient quantities, tears all the outer coating off the diaphragm.

It leaves the epigastric tissue, so I am informed, a useless wreck.

This I don't deny. It gets, they tell me, into the brain. I don't dispute it. It turns the prosencephalon into mere punk. I know it. I've felt it doing it. They tell me – and I believe it – that after even one glass of alcohol, or shall we say Scotch whisky and soda, a man's working power is lowered by twenty per cent. This is a dreadful thing. After three glasses, so it is held, his capacity for sustained rigid thought is cut in two. And after about six glasses the man's working power is reduced by at least a hundred per cent. He merely sits there – in his arm-chair, at his club let us say – with all power, even all *desire* to work gone out of him, not thinking rigidly, not sustaining his thought, a mere shapeless chunk of geniality, half hidden in the blue smoke of his cigar.

Very dreadful, not a doubt. Alcohol is doomed; it is going it is gone. Yet when I think of a hot Scotch on a winter evening, or a Tom Collins on a summer morning, or a gin Rickey beside a tennis-court, or a stein of beer on a bench beside a bowling-green – I wish somehow that we could prohibit the use of alcohol and merely drink beer and whisky and gin as we used to. But these things, it appears, interfere with work. They have got to go.

But turn to the broader and simpler question of WORK itself. In my time one hated it. It was viewed as the natural enemy of man. Now the world has fallen in love with it. My friends, I find, take their deep breathing and their porch sleeping because it makes them work better. They go for a week's vacation in Virginia not for its own sake, but because they say they can work better when they get back. I know a man who wears very loose boots because he can work better in them : and another who wears only soft shirts because he can work better in a soft shirt. There are plenty of men now who would wear dog-harness if they thought they could work more in it. I know another man who walks away out into the country every Sunday : not that he likes the country – he wouldn't recognize a bumble bee if he saw it – but he claims that if he walks on Sunday his head is as clear as a bell for work on Monday.

Against work itself, I say nothing. But I sometimes wonder

if I stand alone in this thing. Am I the only person left who hates it?

Nor is work all. Take food. I admit, here and now, that the lunch I like best – I mean for an ordinary plain lunch, not a party – is a beef steak about one foot square and two inches thick. Can I work on it? No, I can't, but I can work in spite of it. That is as much as one used to ask, twenty-five years ago.

Yet now I find that all my friends boast ostentatiously about the meagre lunch they eat. One tells me that he finds a glass of milk and a prune is quite as much as he cares to take. Another says that a dry biscuit and a glass of water is all that his brain will stand. One lunches on the white of an egg. Another eats merely the yolk. I have only two friends left who can eat a whole egg at a time.

I understand that the fear of these men is that if they eat more than an egg or a biscuit they will feel heavy after lunch. Why they object to feeling heavy, I do not know. Personally, I enjoy it. I like nothing better than to sit round after a heavy lunch with half a dozen heavy friends, smoking heavy cigars. I am well aware that that is wicked. I merely confess the fact. I do not palliate it.

Nor is food all, nor drink, nor work, nor open air. There has spread abroad along with the so-called physical efficiency a perfect passion for *information*. Somehow if a man's stomach is empty and his head clear as a bell, and if he won't drink and won't smoke, he reaches out for information. He wants facts. He reads the newspapers all though, instead of only reading the headings. He clamours for articles filled with statistics about illiteracy and alien immigration and the number of battleships in the Japanese navy.

I know quite a lot of men who have actually bought the new *Encyclopaedia Britannica*. What is more, they *read* the thing. They sit in their apartments at night with a glass of water at their elbow reading the encyclopaedia. They say that it is literally filled with facts. Other men spend their time reading the Statistical Abstract of the United States (they say the figures in it are great) and the Acts of Congress, and the list of Presidents since Washington (or was it Washington?).

Spending their evenings thus, and topping it off with a

cold baked apple, and sleeping out in the snow, they go to work in the morning, so they tell me, with a positive sense of exhilaration. I have no doubt that they do. But, for me, I confess that once and for all I am out of it. I am left behind.

Add to it all such rising dangers as total prohibition, and the female franchise, the daylight saving, and eugenic marriage, together with proportional representation, the initiative and the referendum, and the duty of the citizen to take an intelligent interest in politics – and I admit that I shall not be sorry to go away from here.

But before I *do* go, I have one hope. I understand that down in Hayti things are very different. Bull fights, cock fights, dog fights, are openly permitted. Business never begins till eleven in the morning. Everybody sleeps after lunch, and the bars remain open all night. Marriage is but a casual relation. In fact, the general condition of morality, so they tell me, is lower in Hayti than it has been anywhere since the time of Nero. Me for Hayti.

❧ XIII ❧

The Old, Old Story
of How Five Men
Went Fishing

THIS IS a plain account of a fishing party. It is not a story. There is no plot. Nothing happens in it and nobody is hurt. The only point of this narrative is its peculiar truth. It not only tells what happened to us – the five people concerned in it – but what has happened and is happening to all the other fishing parties that at the season of the year, from Halifax to Idaho, go gliding out on the unruffled surface of our Canadian and American lakes in the still cool of early summer morning.

We decided to go in the early morning because there is a popular belief that the early morning is the right time for bass fishing. The bass is said to bite in the early morning. Perhaps it does. In fact the thing is almost capable of scientific proof. The bass does *not* bite between eight and twelve. It does *not* bite between twelve and six in the afternoon. Nor does it bite between six o'clock and midnight. All these things are known facts. The inference is that the bass bites furiously at about daybreak.

At any rate our party were unanimous about starting early. "Better make an early start," said the Colonel, when the idea of the party was suggested. "Oh, yes," said George Popley, the bank manager, "we want to get right out on the shoal while the fish are biting."

When he said this all our eyes glistened. Everybody's do.

There's a thrill in the words. To "get right out on the shoal at daybreak when the fish are biting," is an idea that goes to any man's brain.

If you listen to the men talking in a Pullman car, or an hotel corridor, or, better still, at the little tables in a first-class bar, you will not listen long before you hear one say: "Well, we got out early, just after sunrise, right on the shoal." And presently, even if you can't hear him, you will see him reach out his two hands and hold them about two feet apart for the other man to admire. He is measuring the fish. No, not the fish they caught; this was the big one that they lost. But they had him right up to the top of the water. Oh, yes, he was up to the top of the water all right. The number of huge fish that have been heaved up to the top of the water in our lakes is almost incredible. Or at least it used to be when we still had bar rooms and little tables for serving that vile stuff Scotch whisky and such foul things as gin Rickeys and John Collinses. It makes one sick to think of it, doesn't it? But there was good fishing in the bars, all the winter.

But, as I say, we decided to go early in the morning. Charlie Jones, the railroad man, said that he remembered how when he was a boy, up in Wisconsin, they used to get out at five in the morning – not get up at five but be on the shoal at five. It appears that there is a shoal somewhere in Wisconsin where the bass lie in thousands. Kernin, the lawyer, said that when he was a boy – this was on Lake Rosseau – they used to get out at four. It seems there is a shoal in Lake Rosseau where you can haul up the bass as fast as you can drop your line. The shoal is hard to find – very hard. Kernin can find it, but it is doubtful – so I gather – if any other living man can. The Wisconsin shoal, too, is very difficult to find. Once you find it, you are all right; but it's hard to find. Charlie Jones can find it. If you were in Wisconsin right now he'd take you straight to it, but probably no other person now alive could reach that shoal. In the same way Colonel Morse knows of a shoal in Lake Simcoe where he used to fish years and years ago and which, I understand, he can still find.

I have mentioned that Kernin is a lawyer, and Jones a

railroad man and Popley a banker. But I needn't have. Any reader would take it for granted. In any fishing party there is always a lawyer. You can tell him at sight. He is the one of the party that has a landing net and a steel rod in sections with a wheel that is used to wind the fish to the top of the water.

And there is always a banker. You can tell him by his good clothes. Popley, in the bank, wears his banking suit. When he goes fishing he wears his fishing suit. It is much the better of the two, because his banking suit has ink marks on it, and his fishing suit has no fish marks on it.

As for the railroad man – quite so, the reader knows it as well as I do – you can tell him because he carries a pole that he cut in the bush himself, with a ten-cent line wrapped round the end of it. Jones says he can catch as many fish with this kind of line as Kernin can with his patent rod and wheel. So he can too. Just the same number.

But Kernin says that with his patent apparatus if you get a fish on you can *play* him. Jones says to Hades with *playing* him : give him a fish on his line and he'll haul him in all right. Kernin says he'd lose him. But Jones says *he* wouldn't. In fact he *guarantees* to haul the fish in. Kernin says that more than once – in Lake Rosseau – he has played a fish for over half an hour. I forget now why he stopped; I think the fish quit playing.

I have heard Kernin and Jones argue this question of their two rods, as to which rod can best pull in the fish, for half an hour. Others may have heard the same question debated. I know no way by which it could be settled.

Our arrangement to go fishing was made at the little golf club of our summer town on the veranda where we sit in the evening. Oh, it's just a little place, nothing pretentious : the links are not much good for *golf*; in fact we don't play much *golf* there, so far as golf goes, and of course, we don't serve meals at the club, it's not like that – and no, we've nothing to drink there because of prohibition. But we go and *sit* there. It is a good place to *sit*, and, after all, what else can you do in the present state of the law?

So it was there that we arranged the party.

The thing somehow seemed to fall into the mood of each of us. Jones said he had been hoping that some of the boys would get up a fishing party. It was apparently the one kind of pleasure that he really cared for. For myself I was delighted to get in with a crowd of regular fishermen like these four, especially as I hadn't been out fishing for nearly ten years, though fishing is a thing I am passionately fond of. I know no pleasure in life like the sensation of getting a four-pound bass on the hook and hauling him up to the top of the water, to weigh him. But, as I say, I hadn't been out for ten years. Oh, yes, I live right beside the water every summer, and yes, certainly – I am saying so – I am passionately fond of fishing, but still somehow I hadn't been *out*. Every fisherman knows just how that happens. The years have a way of slipping by. Yet I must say I was surprised to find that so keen a sport as Jones hadn't been out – so it presently appeared – for eight years. I had imagined he practically lived on the water. And Colonel Morse and Kernin, I was amazed to find, hadn't been out for twelve years, not since the day – so it came out in conversation – when they went out together in Lake Rosseau and Kernin landed a perfect monster, a regular corker, five pounds and a half, they said; or no, I don't think he *landed* him. No, I remember, he didn't *land* him. He caught him – and he *could* have landed him, he should have landed him – but he *didn't* land him. That was it. Yes, I remember Kernin and Morse had a slight discussion about it – oh, perfectly amicable – as to whether Morse had fumbled with the net or whether Kernin – the whole argument was perfectly friendly – had made an ass of himself by not "striking" soon enough. Of course the whole thing was so long ago that both of them could look back on it without any bitterness or ill nature. In fact it amused them. Kernin said it was the most laughable thing he ever saw in his life to see poor old Jack – that's Morse's name – shoving away with the landing net wrong side up. And Morse said he'd never forget seeing poor old Kernin yanking his line first this way and then that and not knowing where to try to haul it. It made him laugh to look back at it.

They might have gone on laughing for quite a time, but Charlie Jones interrupted by saying that in his opinion a landing net is a piece of darned foolishness. Here Popley agrees with him. Kernin objects that if you don't use a net you'll lose your fish at the side of the boat. Jones says no : give **him** a hook well through the fish and a stout line in his hand and that fish has *got* to come in. Popley says so too. He says let him have his hook fast through the fish's head with a short stout line, and put him (Popley) at the other end of that line and that fish will come in. It's *got* to. Otherwise Popley will know why. That's the alternative. Either the fish must come in, or Popley must know why. There's no escape from the logic of it.

But perhaps some of my readers have heard the thing discussed before.

So, as I say, we decided to go the next morning and to make an early start. All of the boys were at one about that. When I say "boys," I use the word, as it is used in fishing, to mean people from say forty-five to sixty-five. There is something about fishing that keeps men young. If a fellow gets out for a good morning's fishing, forgetting all business worries, once in a while — say, once in ten years — it keeps him fresh.

We agreed to go in a launch, a large launch — to be exact, the largest in the town. We could have gone in row boats, but a row boat is a poor thing to fish from. Kernin said that in a row boat it is impossible properly to "*play*" your fish. The side of the boat is so low that the fish is apt to leap over the side into the boat when half "played." Popley said that there is no *comfort* in a row boat. In a launch a man can reach out his feet and take it easy. Charlie Jones said that in a launch a man could rest his back against something, and Morse said that in a launch a man could rest his neck. Young inexperienced boys, in the small sense of the word, never think of these things. So they go out and after a few hours their necks get tired; whereas a group of expert fishers in a launch can rest their backs and necks and even fall asleep during the pauses when the fish stop biting.

Anyway all the "boys" agreed that the great advantage of a launch would be that we could get a *man* to take us. By that means the man could see to getting the worms, and the man would be sure to have spare lines, and the man could come along to our different places — we were all beside the water — and pick us up. In fact the more we thought about the advantage of having a "man" to take us the better we liked it. As a boy gets old he likes to have a man around to do the work.

Anyway Frank Rolls, the man we decided to get, not only has the biggest launch in town but what is more Frank *knows* the lake. We called him up at his boat-house over the phone and said we'd give him five dollars to take us out first thing in the morning provided that he knew the shoal. He said he knew it.

I don't know, to be quite candid about it, who mentioned whisky first. In these days everybody has to be a little careful. I imagine we had all been *thinking* whisky for some time before anybody said it. But there is a sort of convention that when men go fishing they must have whisky. Each man makes the pretence that one thing he needs at six o'clock in the morning is cold raw whisky. It is spoken of in terms of affection. One man says the first thing you need if you're going fishing is a good "snort" of whisky; another says that a good "snifter" is the very thing; and the others agree that no man can fish properly without "a horn," or a "bracer" or an "eye-opener." Each man really decides that he himself won't take any. But he feels that, in a collective sense, the "boys" need it.

So it was with us. The Colonel said he'd bring along "a bottle of booze." Popley said, no, let *him* bring it; Kernin said let him; and Charlie Jones said no, he'd bring it. It turned out that the Colonel had some very good Scotch at his house that he'd like to bring; oddly enough Popley had some good Scotch in *his* house too; and, queer though it is, each of the boys had Scotch in his house. When the discussion closed we knew that each of the five of us was intending to bring a bottle of whisky. Each of the five of us expected the other to drink one and a quarter bottles in the course of the morning.

I suppose we must have talked on that veranda till long after one in the morning. It was probably nearer two than one when we broke up. But we agreed that that made no difference. Popley said that for him three hours' sleep, the right kind of sleep, was far more refreshing than ten. Kernin said that a lawyer learns to snatch his sleep when he can, and

Jones said that in railroad work a man pretty well cuts out sleep.

So we had no alarms whatever about not being ready by five. Our plan was simplicity itself. Men like ourselves in responsible positions learn to organize things easily. In fact Popley says it is that faculty that has put us where we are. So the plan simply was that Frank Rolls should come along at five o'clock and blow his whistle in front of our places, and at that signal each man would come down to his wharf with his rod and kit and so we'd be off to the shoal without a moment's delay.

The weather we ruled out. It was decided that even if it rained that made no difference. Kernin said that fish bite better in the rain. And everybody agreed that man with a couple of snorts in him need have no fear of a little rain water.

So we parted, all keen on the enterprise. Nor do I think even now that there was anything faulty or imperfect in that party as we planned it.

I heard Frank Rolls blowing his infernal whistle opposite my summer cottage at some ghastly hour in the morning. Even without getting out of bed, I could see from the window that it was no day for fishing. No, not raining exactly. I don't mean that, but one of those peculiar days – I don't mean *wind* – there was no wind, but a sort of feeling in the air that showed anybody who understands bass fishing that it was a perfectly rotten day for going out. The fish, I seemed to know it, wouldn't bite.

When I was still fretting over the annoyance of the disappointment I heard Frank Rolls blowing his whistle in front of the other cottages. I counted thirty whistles altogether. Then I fell into a light doze – not exactly sleep, but a sort of *doze* – I can find no other word for it. It was clear to me that the other "boys" had thrown the thing over. There was no use in my trying to go out alone. I stayed where I was, my doze lasting till ten o'clock.

When I walked up town later in the morning I couldn't help being struck by the signs in the butcher's shops and the restaurants, FISH, FRESH FISH, FRESH LAKE FISH.

Where in blazes do they get those fish anyway?

❦XIV❧

Back from the Land

I HAVE just come back now with the closing in of autumn —
to the city. I have hung up my hoe in my study; my spade is
put away behind the piano. I have with me seven pounds of
Paris Green that I had over. Anybody who wants it may have
it. I didn't like to bury it for fear of its poisoning the ground.
I didn't like to throw it away for fear of its destroying cattle.
I was afraid to leave it in my summer place for fear that it
might poison the tramps who generally break in in Novem-
ber. I have it with me now. I move it from room to room, as
I hate to turn my back upon it. Anybody who wants it, I
repeat, can have it.

I should like also to give away, either to the Red Cross or
to anything else, ten packets of radish seed (the early curled
variety, I think), fifteen packets of cucumber seed (the long
succulent variety, I believe it says), and twenty packets of
onion seed (the Yellow Danvers, distinguished, I understand,
for its edible flavour and its nutritious properties). It is not
likely that I shall ever, on this side of the grave, plant onion
seed again. All these things I have with me. My vegetables
are to come after me by freight. They are booked from Simcoe County to Montreal; at present they are, I believe, passing through Schenectady. But they will arrive later all right.
They were seen going through Detroit last week, moving
west. It is the first time that I ever sent anything by freight

anywhere. I never understood before the wonderful organization of the railroads. But they tell me that there is a bad congestion of freight down South this month. If my vegetables get tangled up in that there is no telling when they will arrive.

In other words, I am one of the legion of men – quiet, determined, resolute men – who went out last spring to plant the land, and who are now back.

With me – and I am sure that I speak for all the others as well – it was not a question of mere pleasure; it was no love of gardening for its own sake that inspired us. It was a plain national duty. What we said to ourselves was: "This war has got to stop. The men in the trenches thus far have failed to stop it. Now let *us* try. The whole thing," we argued, "is a plain matter of food production."

"If we raise enough food the Germans are bound to starve. Very good. Let us kill them."

I suppose there was never a more grimly determined set of men went out from the cities than those who went out last May, as I did, to conquer the food problem. I don't mean to say that each and every one of us actually left the city. But we all "went forth" in the metaphorical sense. Some of the men cultivated back gardens; others took vacant lots; some went out into the suburbs; and others, like myself, went right out into the country.

We are now back. Each of us has with him his Paris Green, his hoe and the rest of his radish seed.

The time has, therefore, come for a plain, clear statement of our experience. We have, as everybody knows, failed. We have been beaten back all along the line. Our potatoes are buried in a jungle of autumn burdocks. Our radishes stand seven feet high, uneatable. Our tomatoes, when last seen, were greener than they were at the beginning of August, and getting greener every week. Our celery looked as delicate as a maidenhair fern. Our Indian corn was nine feet high with a tall feathery spike on top of that, but no sign of anything eatable about it from top to bottom.

I look back with a sigh of regret at those bright, early days in April when we were all buying hoes, and talking soil and waiting for the snow to be off the ground. The street cars, as we went up and down to our offices, were a busy babel of garden talk. There was a sort of farmer-like geniality in the air. One spoke freely to strangers. Every man with a hoe was a friend. Men chewed straws in their offices, and kept looking out of windows to pretend to themselves that they were afraid it might blow up rain. "Got your tomatoes in?" one man would ask another as they went up in the elevator. "Yes, I got mine in yesterday," the other would answer, "But I'm just a little afraid that this east wind may blow up a little frost. What we need now is growing weather." And the two men would drift off together from the elevator door along the corridor, their heads together in friendly colloquy.

I have always regarded a lawyer as a man without a soul. There is one who lives next door to me to whom I have not spoken in five years. Yet when I saw him one day last spring heading for the suburbs in a pair of old trousers with a hoe in one hand and a box of celery plants in the other I felt that I loved the man. I used to think that stock-brokers were mere sordid calculating machines. Now that I have seen whole firms of them busy at the hoe, wearing old trousers that reached to their armpits and were tied about the waist with a polka dot necktie, I know that they are men. I know that there are warm hearts beating behind those trousers.

Old trousers, I say. Where on earth did they all come from in such a sudden fashion last spring? Everybody had them. Who would suspect that a man drawing a salary of ten thousand a year was keeping in reserve a pair of pepper-and-salt breeches, four sizes too large for him, just in case a war should break out against Germany! Talk of German mobilization! I doubt whether the organizing power was all on their side after all. At any rate it is estimated that fifty thousand pairs of old trousers were mobilized in Montreal in one week.

But perhaps it was not a case of mobilization, or deliberate preparedness. It was rather an illustration of the primitive instinct that is in all of us and that will out in "war time." Any man worth the name would wear old breeches all the time if the world would let him. Any man will wind a polka dot tie round his waist in preference to wearing patent braces. The makers of the ties know this. That is why they make the tie four feet long. And in the same way if any manufacturer of hats will put on the market an old fedora, with a limp rim and a mark where the ribbon used to be but is not – a hat guaranteed to be six years old, well weathered, well rained on, and certified to have been walked over by a herd of cattle – that man will make and deserve a fortune.

These at least were the fashions of last May. Alas, where are they now? The men that wore them have relapsed again into tailor-made tweeds. They have put on hard new hats. They are shining their boots again. They are shaving again, not merely on Saturday night, but every day. They are sinking back into civilization.

Yet those were bright times and I cannot forbear to linger on them. Nor the least pleasant feature was our rediscovery of the morning. My neighbour on the right was always up at five. My neighbour on the left was out and about by four. With the earliest light of day, little columns of smoke rose along our street from the kitchen ranges where our wives were making coffee for us before the servants got up. By six o'clock the street was alive and busy with friendly salutations. The milkman seemed a late comer, a poor, sluggish fellow who failed to appreciate the early hours of the day. A man, we found, might live through quite a little Iliad of adventure before going to his nine o'clock office.

"How will you possibly get time to put in a garden?" I asked of one of my neighbours during this glad period of early spring before I left for the country. "Time!" he exclaimed. "Why, my dear fellow, I don't have to be down at the warehouse till eight-thirty."

Later in the summer I saw the wreck of his garden, choked with weeds. "Your garden," I said, "is in poor shape." "Garden!" he said indignantly. "How on earth can I find time for a garden? Do you realize that I have to be down at the warehouse at eight-thirty?"

When I look back to our bright beginnings our failure seems hard indeed to understand. It is only when I survey the whole garden movement in melancholy retrospect that I am able to see some of the reasons for it.

The principal one, I think, is the question of the season. It appears that the right time to begin gardening is last year. For many things it is well to begin the year before last. For good results one must begin even sooner. Here, for example, are the directions, as I interpret them, for growing asparagus. Having secured a suitable piece of ground, preferably a deep friable loam rich in nitrogen, go out three years ago and plough or dig deeply. Remain a year inactive, thinking. Two years ago pulverize the soil thoroughly. Wait a year. As soon as last year comes set out the young shoots. Then spend a quiet winter doing nothing. The asparagus will then be ready to work at *this* year.

This is the rock on which we were wrecked. Few of us were men of sufficient means to spend several years in quiet thought waiting to begin gardening. Yet that is, it seems, the only way to begin. Asparagus demands a preparation of four years. To fit oneself to grow strawberries requires three years. Even for such humble things as peas, beans, and lettuce the instructions inevitably read, "plough the soil deeply in the preceeding autumn." This sets up a dilemma. *Which* is the preceeding autumn? If a man begins gardening in the spring he is too late for last autumn and too early for this. On the other hand if he begins in the autumn he is again too late; he has missed this summer's crop. It is, therefore, ridiculous to begin in the autumn and impossible to begin in the spring.

This was our first difficulty. But the second arose from the question of the soil itself. All the books and instructions insist that the selection of the soil is the most important part of gardening. No doubt it is. But, if a man has already selected his own backyard before he opens the book, what remedy is there? All the books lay stress on the need of "a deep, friable loam full of nitrogen." This I have never seen. My own plot of land I found on examination to contain nothing but earth. I could see no trace of nitrogen. I do not deny the existence of loam. There may be such a thing. But I am admitting now in all humility of mind that I don't know what loam is. Last spring my fellow gardeners and I all talked freely of the desirability of "a loam." My own opinion is that none of them had any clearer ideas about it than I had. Speaking from experience, I should say that the only soils are earth, mud and dirt. There are no others.

But I leave out the soil. In any case we were mostly forced to disregard it. Perhaps a more fruitful source of failure even than the lack of loam was the attempt to apply calculation and mathematics to gardening. Thus, if one cabbage will grow in one square foot of ground, how many cabbages will grow in ten square feet of ground? Ten? Not at all. The answer is *one*. You will find as a matter of practical experience that however many cabbages you plant in a garden plot there will be only *one* that will really grow. This you will presently come to speak of as *the* cabbage. Beside it all the others (till the caterpillars finally finish their existence) will look but poor, lean things. But *the* cabbage will be a source of pride and an object of display to visitors; in fact it would ultimately have grown to be a *real* cabbage, such as you buy for ten cents at any market, were it not that you inevitably cut it and eat it when it is still only half-grown.

This always happens to the one cabbage that is of decent size, and to the one tomato that shows signs of turning red (it is really a feeble green-pink), and to the only melon that might have lived to ripen. They get eaten. No one but a practised professional gardener can live and sleep beside a melon three-quarters ripe and a cabbage two-thirds grown without going out and tearing it off the stem.

Even at that it is not a bad plan to eat the stuff while you can. The most peculiar thing about gardening is that all of a sudden everything is too old to eat. Radishes change over night from delicate young shoots not large enough to put on the table into huge plants seven feet high with a root like an Irish shillelagh. If you take your eyes off a lettuce bed for a week the lettuces, not ready to eat when you last looked at them, have changed into a tall jungle of hollyhocks. Green peas are only really green for about two hours. Before that they are young peas; after that they are old peas. Cucumbers are the worst case of all. They change overnight, from delicate little bulbs obviously too slight and dainty to pick, to old cases of yellow leather filled with seeds.

If I were ever to garden again, a thing which is out of the bounds of possibility, I should wait until a certain day and hour when all the plants were ripe, and then go out with a gun and shoot them all dead, so that they could grow no more.

But calculation, I repeat, is the bane of gardening. I knew, among our group of food producers, a party of young engineers, college men, who took an empty farm north of the city as the scene of their summer operations. They took their coats off and applied college methods. They ran out, first, a base line AB, and measured off from it lateral spurs MN, OP, QR, and so on. From these they took side angles with a theodolite so as to get the edges of each of the separate plots of their land absolutely correct. I saw them working at it all through one Saturday afternoon in May. They talked as they did it of the peculiar ignorance of the so-called practical farmer. He never – so they agreed – uses his head. He never – I think I have their phrase correct – stops to think. In laying out his ground for use, it never occurs to him to try to get the maximum result from a given space. If a farmer would only realize that the contents of a circle represent the maximum of space enclosable in a given perimeter, and that a circle is merely a function of its own radius, what a lot of time he would save.

These young men that I speak of laid out their field engineer-fashion with little white posts at even distances. They made a blueprint of the whole thing as they planted it. Every corner of it was charted out. The yield was calculated to a nicety. They had allowed for the fact that some of the stuff might fail to grow by introducing what they called "a coefficient of error." By means of this and by reducing the variation of autumn prices to a mathematical curve, those men not only knew already in the middle of May the exact yield of their farm to within half a bushel (they allowed, they said, a variation of half a bushel per fifty acres), but they knew beforehand within a few cents the market value that they would receive. The figures, as I remember them, were simply amazing. It seemed incredible that fifty acres could produce so much. Yet there were the plain facts in front of one, calculated out. The thing amounted practically to a revolution in farming. At least it ought to have. And it would have if those young men had come again to hoe their field. But it turned out, most unfortunately, that they were busy. To their great regret they were too busy to come. They had been working under a free-and-easy arrangement. Each man was to give what time he could every Saturday. It was left to every man's honour to do what he could. There was no compulsion. Each man trusted the others to be there. In fact the thing was not only an experiment in food production, it was also a new departure in social co-operation. The first

Saturday that those young men worked there were, so I have been told, seventy-five of them driving in white stakes and running lines. The next Saturday there were fifteen of them planting potatoes. The rest were busy. The week after that there was one man hoeing weeds. After that silence fell upon the deserted garden, broken only by the cry of the chick-a-dee and the choo-choo feeding on the waving heads of the thistles.

But I have indicated only two or three of the ways of failing at food production. There are ever so many more. What amazes me, in returning to the city, is to find the enormous quantities of produce of all sorts offered for sale in the markets. It is an odd thing that last spring, by a queer oversight, we never thought, any of us, of this process of increasing the supply. If every patriotic man would simply take a large basket and go to the market every day and buy all that he could carry away there need be no further fear of a food famine.

And, meantime, my own vegetables are on their way. They are in a soap box with bars across the top, coming by freight. They weigh forty-six pounds, including the box. They represent the result of four months' arduous toil in sun, wind, and storm. Yet it is pleasant to think that I shall be able to feed with them some poor family of refugees during the rigour of the winter. Either that or give them to the hens. I certainly won't eat the rotten things myself.

❧XV❧

The Perplexity Column
as Done by
the Jaded Journalist

INSTANTANEOUS ANSWERS TO ALL QUESTIONS

*(All questions written out legibly with the name and address of
the sender and accompanied by one dollar, answered immediately
and without charge.)*

Harvard Student asks:

Can you tell me the date at which, or on which, Oliver
Cromwell's father died?

Answer. No, I can't.

Student of Mathematics asks:

Will you kindly settle a matter involving a wager between
myself and a friend? A. bet B. that a pedestrian in walking
downhill over a given space and alternately stepping with
either foot, covers more ground than a man coasting over the
same road on a bicycle. Which of us wins?

Answer. I don't understand the question, and I don't know
which of you is A.

Chess-player asks:

Is the Knight's gambit recognized now as a permissible
opening in chess?

Answer. I don't play chess.

Reuben Boob asks:

For some time past I have been calling upon a young lady friend at her house evenings and going out with her to friends' nights. I should like to know if it would be all right to ask to take her alone with me to the theatre?

Answer. Certainly not. This column is very strict about these things. Not alone. Not for a moment. It is better taste to bring your father with you.

Auction asks:

In playing bridge please tell me whether the third or the second player ought to discard from weakness on a long suit when trumps have been twice round and the lead is with dummy.

Answer. Certainly.

Lady of Society asks:

Can you tell me whether the widow of a marquis is entitled to go in to dinner before the eldest daughter of an earl?

Answer. Ha! ha! This is a thing we know – something that we *do* know. You put your foot in it when you asked us that. We have *lived* this sort of thing too long ever to make any error. The widow of a marquis, whom you should by rights call a marchioness dowager (but we overlook it – you meant no harm) is entitled (in any hotel that we know or frequent) to go in to dinner whenever, and as often, as she likes. On a dining-car the rule is the other way.

Vassar Girl asks:

What is the date of the birth of Caracalla?
Answer. I couldn't say.

Lexicographer asks:

Can you tell me the proper way to spell "dog"?
Answer. Certainly. "Dog" should be spelt, properly and precisely, "dog." When it is used in the sense to mean not "*a* dog" or "*one* dog" but two or more dogs – in other words what we grammarians are accustomed to call the plural – it

is proper to add to it the diphthong, *s*, pronounced with a hiss like z in soup.

But for all these questions of spelling your best plan is to buy a copy of Our Standard Dictionary, published in ten volumes, by this newspaper, at forty dollars.

Ignoramus asks:

Can you tell me how to spell "cat"?

Answer. Didn't you hear what we just said about how to spell "dog"? Buy the Dictionary.

Careworn Mother asks:

I am most anxious to find out the relation of the earth's diameter to its circumference. Can you, or any of your readers, assist me in it?

Answer. The earth's circumference is estimated to be three decimal one four one five nine of its diameter, a fixed relation indicated by the Greek letter *pi*. If you like we will tell you what *pi* is. Shall we?

"Brink of Suicide" writes:

Can you, will you, tell me what is the Sanjak of Novi Bazar?

Answer. The Sanjak of Novi Bazar is bounded on the north by its northern frontier, cold and cheerless, and covered during the winter with deep snow. The east of the Sanjak occupies a more easterly position. Here the sun rises – at first slowly, but gathering speed as it goes. After having traversed the entire width of the whole Sanjak, the magnificent orb, slowly and regretfully, sinks into the west. On the south, where the soil is more fertile and where the land begins to be worth occupying, the Sanjak is, or will be, bounded by the British Empire.

✠XVI✠

Simple Stories of Success,

or

How to Succeed in Life

LET me begin with a sort of parable. Many years ago when I was on the staff of a great public school, we engaged a new swimming master.

He was the most successful man in that capacity that we had had for years.

Then one day it was discovered that he couldn't swim.

He was standing at the edge of the swimming tank explaining the breast stroke to the boys in the water.

He lost his balance and fell in. He was drowned.

Or no, he wasn't drowned, I remember, – he was rescued by some of the pupils whom he had taught to swim.

After he was resuscitated by the boys – it was one of the things he had taught them – the school dismissed him.

Then some of the boys who were sorry for him taught him how to swim, and he got a new job as a swimming master in another place.

But this time he was an utter failure. He swam well, but they said he couldn't *teach*.

So his friends looked about to get him a new job. This was just at the time when the bicycle craze came in. They soon found the man a position as an instructor in bicycle riding. As he had never been on a bicycle in his life, he made an admirable teacher. He stood fast on the ground and said, "Now then, all you need is confidence."

Then one day he got afraid that he might be found out. So he went out to a quiet place and got on a bicycle, at the top of a slope, to learn to ride it. The bicycle ran away with him. But for the skill and daring of one of his pupils, who saw him and rode after him, he would have been killed.

This story, as the reader sees, is endless. Suffice it to say that the man I speak of is now in an aviation school teaching people to fly. They say he is one of the best aviators that ever walked.

According to all the legends and story books, the principal factor in success is perseverance. Personally, I think there is nothing in it. If anything, the truth lies the other way.

There is an old motto that runs, "If at first you don't succeed, try, try again." This is nonsense. It ought to read, "If at first you don't succeed, quit, quit, at once."

If you can't do a thing, more or less, the first time you try, you will never do it. Try something else while there is yet time.

Let me illustrate this with a story.

I remember, long years ago, at a little school that I attended in the country, we had a schoolmaster, who used perpetually to write on the blackboard, in a copperplate hand, the motto that I have just quoted:

> "If at first you don't succeed,
> Try, try, again."

He wore plain clothes and had a hard, determined face. He was studying for some sort of preliminary medical examination, and was saving money for a medical course. Every now and then he went away to the city and tried the examination: and he always failed. Each time he came back, he would write up on the blackboard:

> "Try, try again."

And always he looked grimmer and more determined than before. The strange thing was that, with all his industry and determination, he would break out every now and then into drunkenness, and lie round the tavern at the crossroads, and the school would be shut for two days. Then he came back, more fiercely resolute than ever. Even children could see that the man's life was a fight. It was like the battle between Good and Evil in Milton's epics.

Well, after he had tried it four times, the schoolmaster at last passed the examination; and he went away to the city in a suit of store clothes, with eight hundred dollars that he had saved up, to study medicine. Now it happened that he had a brother who was not a bit like himself, but was a sort of ne'er-do-well, always hard-up and sponging on other people, and never working.

And when the schoolmaster came to the city and his brother knew that he had eight hundred dollars, he came to him and got him drinking and persuaded him to hand over the eight hundred dollars and to let him put it into the Louisiana State lottery. In those days the Louisiana Lottery had not yet been forbidden the use of the mails, and you could buy a ticket for anything from one dollar up. The Grand Prize was two hundred thousand dollars, and the Seconds were a hundred thousand each.

So the brother persuaded the schoolmaster to put the money in. He said he had a system for buying only the tickets with prime numbers, that won't divide by anything, and that it must win. He said it was a mathematical certainty, and he figured it out with the schoolmaster in the back room of a saloon, with a box of dominoes on the table to show the plan of it. He told the schoolmaster that he himself would only take ten per cent of what they made, as a commission for showing the system, and the schoolmaster could have the rest.

So, in a mad moment, the schoolmaster handed over his roll of money, and that was the last he ever saw of it.

The next morning when he was up he was fierce with rage and remorse for what he had done. He could not go back to the school, and he had no money to go forward. So he stayed where he was in the little hotel where he had got drunk, and went on drinking. He looked so fierce and unkempt that in the hotel they were afraid of him, and the bar-tenders watched him out of the corners of their eyes wondering what he would do; because they knew that there was only one end possible, and they waited for it to come. And presently it came. One of the bar-tenders went up to the schoolmaster's room to bring up a letter, and he found him lying on the bed with his face grey as ashes, and his eyes looking up at the ceiling. He was stone dead. Life had beaten him.

And the strange thing was that the letter that the bar-tender carried up that morning was from the management of the Louisiana Lottery. It contained a draft on New York, signed by the treasurer of the State of Louisiana, for two hundred thousand dollars. The schoolmaster had won the Grand Prize.

The above story, I am afraid, is a little gloomy. I put it down merely for the moral it contained, and I became so absorbed in telling it that I almost forgot what the moral was that it was meant to convey. But I think the idea is that if the schoolmaster had long before abandoned the study of medicine, for which he was not fitted, and gone in, let us say, for playing the banjo, he might have become end-man in a minstrel show. Yes, that was it.

Let me pass on to other elements in success.

I suppose that anybody will admit that the peculiar quality that is called initiative – the ability to act promptly on one's own judgement – is a factor of the highest importance.

I have seen this illustrated two or three times in a very striking fashion.

I knew, in Toronto – it is long years ago – a singularly bright young man whose name was Robinson. He had had some training in the iron and steel business, and when I knew him was on the look out for an opening.

I met him one day in a great hurry, with a valise in his hand.

"Where are you going?" I asked.

"Over to England," he said. "There is a firm in Liverpool that have advertised that they want an agent here, and I'm going over to apply for the job."

"Can't you do it by letter?" I asked.

"That's just it," said Robinson, with a chuckle, "all the other men will apply by letter. I'll go right over myself and get there as soon or sooner than the letters. I'll be the man on the spot, and I'll get the job."

He was quite right. He went over to Liverpool, and was back in a fortnight with English clothes and a big salary.

But I cannot recommend his story to my friends. In fact, it should not be told too freely. It is apt to be dangerous.

I remember once telling this story of Robinson to a young man called Tomlinson who was out of a job. Tomlinson had a head two sizes too big, and a face like a bun. He had lost three jobs in a bank and two in a broker's office, but he knew his work, and on paper he looked a good man.

I told him about Robinson, to encourage him, and the story made a great impression.

"Say, that was a great scheme, eh?" he kept repeating. He had no command of words, and always said the same thing over and over.

A few days later I met Tomlinson in the street with a valise in his hand.

"Where are you going?" I asked.

"I'm off to Mexico," he answered. "They're advertising for a Canadian teller for a bank in Tuscapulco. I've sent my credentials down, and I'm going to follow them right up in person. In a thing like this, the personal element is everything."

So Tomlinson went down to Mexico and he travelled by sea to Mexico City, and then with a mule train to Tuscapulco. But the mails, with his credentials, went by land and got there two days ahead of him.

When Tomlinson got to Tuscapulco he went into the bank and he spoke to the junior manager and told him what he came for. "I'm awfully sorry," the junior manager said, "I'm afraid that this post has just been filled." Then he went into an inner room to talk with the manager. "The tellership that you wanted a Canadian for," he asked, "didn't you say that you have a man already?"

"Yes," said the manager, "a brilliant young fellow from Toronto; his name is Tomlinson, I have his credentials here – a first-class man. I've wired him to come right along, at our expense, and we'll keep the job open for him ten days."

"There's a young man outside," said the junior, "who wants to apply for the job."

"Outside?" exclaimed the manager. "How did he get here?"

"Came in on the mule train this morning: says he can do the work and wants the job."

"What's he like?" asked the manager.

The junior shook his head.

"Pretty dusty looking customer," he said. "Shifty looking."

"Same old story," murmured the manager. "It's odd how these fellows drift down here, isn't it? Up to something crooked at home, I suppose. Understands the working of a bank, eh? I guess he understands it a little too well for my taste. No, no," he continued, tapping the papers that lay on the table, "now that we've got a first-class man like Tomlinson, let's hang on to him. We can easily wait ten days, and the cost of the journey is nothing to the bank as compared with getting a man of Tomlinson's stamp. And, by the way, you might telephone to the Chief of Police and get him to see to it that this loafer gets out of town straight off."

So the Chief of Police shut up Tomlinson in the calaboose and then sent him down to Mexico City under a guard. By the time the police were done with him he was dead broke, and it took him four months to get back to Toronto; when he got there, the place in Mexico had been filled long ago.

But I can imagine that some of my readers might suggest that I have hitherto been dealing only with success in a very limited way, and that more interest would lie in discussing how the really great fortunes are made.

Everybody feels an instictive interest in knowing how our great captains of industry, our financiers and railroad magnates made their money.

Here the explanation is really a very simple one. There is, in fact, only one way to amass a huge fortune in business or railway management. One must begin at the bottom. One must mount the ladder from the lowest rung. But this lowest rung is everything. Any man who can stand upon it with his foot well poised, his head erect, his arms braced and his eye directed upward, will inevitably mount to the top.

But after all — I say this as a kind of afterthought in conclusion — why bother with success at all? I have observed that the successful people get very little real enjoyment out of life. In fact the contrary is true. If I had to choose — with an eye to having a really pleasant life — between success and ruin, I should prefer ruin every time. I have several friends who are completely ruined – some two or three times – in a large way of course; and I find that if I want to get a really good dinner, where the champagne is just as it ought to be, and where hospitality is unhindered by mean thoughts of expense, I can get it best at the house of a ruined man.

❧XVII❧

In Dry Toronto

A LOCAL STUDY OF A UNIVERSAL TOPIC

Note. – Our readers – our numerous readers – who live in Equatorial Africa, may read this under the title "In Dry Timbucto"; those who live in Central America will kindly call it "In Dry Tehauntepec."

IT may have been, for aught I know, the change from a wet to a dry atmosphere. I am told that, biologically, such things profoundly affect the human system.

At any rate I found it impossible that night – I was on the train from Montreal to Toronto – to fall asleep.

A peculiar wakefulness seemed to have seized upon me, which appeared, moreover, to afflict the other passengers as well. In the darkness of the car I could distinctly hear them groaning at intervals.

"Are they ill?" I asked, through the curtains, of the porter as he passed.

"No, sir," he said, "they're not ill. Those is the Toronto passengers."

"All in this car?" I asked.

"All except that gen'lman you may have heard singing in the smoking compartment. He's booked through to Chicago."

But, as is usual in such cases, sleep came at last with unusual heaviness. I seemed obliterated from the world till, all of a sudden, I found myself, as it were, up and dressed and seated in the observation car at the back of the train, awaiting my arrival.

"Is this Toronto?" I asked of the Pullman conductor, as I peered through the window of the car.

The conductor rubbed the pane with his finger and looked out.

"I think so," he said.

"Do we stop here?" I asked.

"I think we do this morning," he answered. "I think I heard the conductor say that they have a lot of milk cans to put off here this morning. I'll just go and find out, sir."

"Stop here!" broke in an irascible-looking gentleman in a grey tweed suit who was sitting in the next chair to mine. "Do they *stop* here? I should say they did indeed. Don't you know," he added, turning to the Pullman conductor, "that any train is *compelled* to stop here. There's a by-law, a municipal by-law of the City of Toronto, *compelling* every train to stop?"

"I didn't know it," said the conductor humbly.

"Do you mean to say," continued the irascible gentleman, "that you have never read the by-laws of the City of Toronto?"

"No, sir," said the conductor.

"The ignorance of these fellows," said the man in grey tweed, swinging his chair round again towards me. "We ought to have a by-law to compel them to read the by-laws. I must start an agitation for it at once." Here he took out a little red notebook and wrote something in it, murmuring, "We need a new agitation anyway."

Presently he shut the book up with a snap. I noticed that there was a sort of peculiar alacrity in everything he did.

"You, sir," he said, "have, of course, read our municipal by-laws?"

"Oh, yes," I answered. "Splendid, aren't they? They read like a romance."

"You are most flattering to our city," said the irascible gentleman with a bow. "Yet you, sir, I take it, are not from Toronto."

"No," I answered, as humbly as I could. "I'm from Montreal."

"Ah!" said the gentleman, as he sat back and took a thorough look at me. "From Montreal? Are you drunk?"

"No," I replied. "I don't think so."

"But you are *suffering* for a drink," said my new acquaintance eagerly. "You need it, eh? You feel already a kind of craving, eh what?"

"No," I answered. "The fact is it's rather early in the morning —"

"Quite so," broke in the irascible gentleman, "but I understand that in Montreal all the saloons are open at seven, and even at that hour are crowded, sir, crowded."

I shook my head.

"I think that has been exaggerated," I said. "In fact, we always try to avoid crowding and jostling as far as possible. It is generally understood, as a matter of politeness, that the first place in the line is given to the clergy, the Board of Trade, and the heads of the universities."

"Is it conceivable!" said the gentleman in grey. "One moment, please, till I make a note. 'All clergy – I think you said *all*, did you not? – drunk at seven in the morning.' Deplorable! But here we are at the Union Station – commodious, is it not? Justly admired, in fact, all over the known world. Observe," he continued as we alighted from the train and made our way into the station, "the upstairs and the downstairs, connected by flights of stairs; quite unique and most convenient: if you don't meet your friends downstairs all you have to do is to look upstairs. If they are not there, you simply come down again. But stop, you are going to walk up the street? I'll go with you."

At the outer door of the station – just as I had remembered it – stood a group of hotel bus-men and porters.

But how changed!

They were like men blasted by a great sorrow. One, with his back turned, was leaning against a post, his head buried on his arm.

"Prince George Hotel," he groaned at intervals. "Prince George Hotel."

Another was bending over a little handrail, his head sunk, his arms almost trailing to the ground.

"*King Edward*," he sobbed, "*King Edward*."

A third, seated on a stool, looked feebly up, with tears visible in his eyes.

"Walker House," he moaned. "First-class accommodation for —" then he broke down and cried.

"Take this handbag," I said to one of the men, "to the *Prince George*."

The man ceased his groaning for a moment and turned to me with something like passion.

"Why do you come to *us*?" he protested. "Why not go to one of the others. Go to *him*," he added, as he stirred with his foot a miserable being who lay huddled on the ground and murmured at intervals, "*Queen's*! Queen's Hotel."

But my new friend, who stood at my elbow, came to my rescue.

"Take his bags," he said, "you've got to. You know the by-law. Take it or I'll call a policeman. You know *me*. My name's Narrowpath. I'm on the council."

The man touched his hat and took the bag with a murmured apology.

"Come along," said my companion, whom I now perceived to be a person of dignity and civic importance. "I'll walk up with you, and show you the city as we go."

We had hardly got well upon the street before I realized the enormous change that total prohibition had effected. Everywhere were the bright smiling faces of working people, laughing and singing at their tasks, and, early though it was, cracking jokes and asking one another riddles as they worked.

I noticed one man, evidently a city employé, in a rough white suit, busily cleaning the street with a broom and singing to himself: "How does the little busy bee improve the shining hour." Another employé, who was handling a little hose, was singing, "Little drops of water, little grains of sand, Tra, la, la, la, *la* la, Prohibition's grand."

"Why do they sing?" I asked. "Are they crazy?"

"Sing?" said Mr Narrowpath. "They can't help it. They haven't had a drink of whisky for four months."

A coal cart went by with a driver, no longer grimy and smudged, but neatly dressed with a high white collar and a white silk tie.

My companion pointed at him as he passed.

"Hasn't had a glass of beer for four months," he said. "Notice the difference. That man's work is now a pleasure to him. He used to spend all his evenings sitting round in the back parlours of the saloons beside the stove. Now what do you think he does?"

"I have no idea."

"Loads up his cart with coal and goes for a drive – out in the country. Ah, sir, you who live still under the curse of the whisky traffic little know what a pleasure work itself becomes when drink and all that goes with it is eliminated. Do you see that man, on the other side of the street, with the tool bag?"

"Yes," I said, "a plumber, is he not?"

"Exactly, a plumber. Used to drink heavily – couldn't keep a job more than a week. Now, you can't drag him from his work. Came to my house to fix a pipe under the kitchen sink – wouldn't quit at six o'clock. Got in under the sink and begged to be allowed to stay – said he hated to go home. We had to drag him out with a rope. But here we are at your hotel."

We entered.

But how changed the place seemed.

Our feet echoed on the flagstones of the deserted rotunda.

At the office desk sat a clerk, silent and melancholy, reading the Bible. He put a marker in the book and closed it, murmuring "Leviticus Two."

Then he turned to us.

"Can I have a room," I asked, "on the first floor?"

A tear welled up into the clerk's eye.

"You can have the whole first floor," he said, and he added, with a half sob, "and the second, too, if you like."

I could not help contrasting his manner with what it was in the old days, when the mere mention of a room used to throw him into a fit of passion, and when he used to tell me that I could have a cot on the roof till Tuesday, and after that, perhaps, a bed in the stable.

Things had changed indeed.

"Can I get breakfast in the grill room?" I inquired of the melancholy clerk.

He shook his head sadly.

"There is no grill room," he answered. "What would you like?"

"Oh, some sort of eggs," I said, "and —"

The clerk reached down below his desk and handed me a hard-boiled egg with the shell off.

142

"Here's your egg," he said. "And there's ice water there at the end of the desk."

He sat back in his chair and went on reading.

"You don't understand," said Mr Narrowpath, who still stood at my elbow. "All that elaborate grill room breakfast business was just a mere relic of the drinking days – sheer waste of time and loss of efficiency. Go on and eat your egg. Eaten it? Now, don't you feel efficient? What more do you want? Comfort, you say? My dear sir! more men have been ruined by comfort – Great heavens, comfort! The most dangerous, deadly drug that ever undermined the human race. But, here, drink your water. Now you're ready to go and do your business, if you have any."

"But," I protested, "it's still only half-past seven in the morning – no offices will be open —"

"Open!" exclaimed Mr. Narrowpath. "Why! they all open at daybreak now."

I had, it is true, a certain amount of business before me, though of no very intricate or elaborate kind – a few simple arrangements with the head of a publishing house such as it falls to my lot to make every now and then. Yet in the old and unregenerate days it used to take all day to do it: the wicked thing that we used to call a comfortable breakfast in the hotel grill room somehow carried one on to about ten o'clock in the morning. Breakfast brought with it the need of a cigar for digestion's sake and with that, for very restfulness, a certain perusal of the *Toronto Globe*, properly corrected and rectified by a look through the *Toronto Mail*. After that it had been my practice to stroll along to my publishers' office at about eleven-thirty, transact my business, over a cigar, with the genial gentleman at the head of it, and then accept his invitation to lunch, with the feeling that a man who has put in a hard and strenuous morning's work is entitled to a few hours of relaxation.

I am inclined to think that in those reprehensible bygone times, many other people did their business in this same way.

"I don't think," I said to Mr. Narrowpath musingly, "that my publisher will be up as early as this. He's a comfortable sort of man."

"Nonsense!" said Mr. Narrowpath. "Not at work at half-past seven! In Toronto! The thing's absurd. Where is the office? Richmond Street? Come along, I'll go with you. I've always a great liking for attending to other people's business."

"I see you have," I said.

"It's our way here," said Mr. Narrowpath with a wave of his hand. "Every man's business, as we see it, is everybody else's business. Come along, you'll be surprised how quickly your business will be done."

Mr. Narrowpath was right.

My publishers' office, as we entered it, seemed a changed place. Activity and efficiency were stamped all over it. My good friend the publisher was not only there, but there with his coat off, inordinately busy, bawling orders – evidently meant for a printing room – through a speaking tube. "Yes," he was shouting, "put WHISKY in black letter capitals, old English, double size, set it up to look attractive, with the legend MADE IN TORONTO in long clear type underneath —"

"Excuse me," he said, as he broke off for a moment. "We've a lot of stuff going through the press this morning – a big distillery catalogue that we are rushing through. We're doing all we can, Mr. Narrowpath," he continued, speaking with the deference due to a member of the City Council, "to boom Toronto as a Whisky Centre."

"Quite right, quite right!" said my companion, rubbing his hands.

"And now, professor," added the publisher, speaking with rapidity, "your contract is all here – only needs signing. I won't keep you more than a moment – write your name here. Miss Sniggins will you please witness this so help you God how's everything in Montreal good morning."

"Pretty quick, wasn't it?" said Mr. Narrowpath, as we stood in the street again.

"Wonderful!" I said, feeling almost dazed. "Why, I shall be able to catch the morning train back again to Montreal —"

"Precisely. Just what everybody finds. Business done in no time. Men who used to spend whole days here clear out now in fifteen minutes. I knew a man whose business efficiency has so increased under our new regime that he says he wouldn't spend more than five minutes in Toronto if he were paid to."

"But what is this?" I asked as we were brought to a pause in our walk at a street crossing by a great block of vehicles. "What are all these drays? Surely, those look like barrels of whisky!"

"So they are," said Mr. Narrowpath proudly. "*Export* whisky. Fine sight, isn't it? Must be what? – twenty – twenty-five – loads of it. This place, sir, mark my words, is going to prove, with its new energy and enterprise, one of the greatest seats of the distillery business, in fact, *the* whisky capital of the North —"

"But I thought," I interrupted, much puzzled, "that whisky was prohibited here since last September?"

"Export whisky – *export*, my dear sir," corrected Mr. Narrowpath. "We don't interfere, we have never, so far as I know, proposed to interfere with any man's right to make and export whisky. That, sir, is a plain matter of business; morality doesn't enter into it."

"I see," I answered. "But will you please tell me what is the meaning of this other crowd of drays coming in the opposite direction? Surely, those are beer barrels, are they not?"

"In a sense they are," admitted Mr. Narrowpath. "That is, they are *import* beer. It comes in from some other province. It was, I imagine, made in this city (our breweries, sir, are second to none), but the sin of *selling* it" – here Mr. Narrowpath raised his hat from his head and stood for a moment in a reverential attitude – "rests on the heads of others."

The press of vehicles had now thinned out and we moved on, my guide still explaining in some detail the distinction between business principles and moral principles, between whisky as a curse and whisky as a source of profit, which I found myself unable to comprehend.

At length I ventured to interrupt.

"Yet it seems almost a pity," I said, "that with all this beer and whisky around an unregenerate sinner like myself should be prohibited from getting a drink."

"A drink!" exclaimed Mr. Narrowpath. "Well, I should say so. Come right in here. You can have anything you want."

We stepped through a street door into a large, long room.

"Why," I exclaimed in surprise, "this is a bar!"

"Nonsense!" said my friend. "The *bar* in this province is forbidden. We've done with the foul thing for ever. This is an Import Shipping Company's Delivery Office."

"But this long counter —"

"It's not a counter, it's a desk."

"And that bar-tender in his white jacket —"

"Tut! Tut! He's not a bar-tender. He's an Import Goods Delivery Clerk."

"What'll you have, gentlemen," said the Import Clerk, polishing a glass as he spoke.

"Two whisky and sodas," said my friend, "long ones."

The Import Clerk mixed the drinks and set them on the desk.

I was about to take one, but he interrupted.

"One minute, sir," he said.

Then he took up a desk telephone that stood beside him and I heard him calling up Montreal. "Hullo, Montreal! Is that Montreal? Well, say, I've just received an offer here for two whisky and sodas at sixty cents, shall I close with it? All right, gentlemen, Montreal has effected the sale. There you are."

"Dreadful, isn't it?" said Mr. Narrowpath. "The sunken, depraved condition of your City of Montreal; actually *selling* whisky. Deplorable!" and with that he buried his face in the bubbles of the whisky and soda.

"Mr. Narrowpath," I said, "would you mind telling me something? I fear I am a little confused, after what I have seen here, as to what your new legislation has been. You have *not* then, I understand, prohibited the making of whisky?"

"Oh, no, we see no harm in that."

"Nor the sale of it?"

"Certainly not," said Mr. Narrowpath, "not if sold *properly*."

"Nor the drinking of it?"

"Oh, no, that least of all. We attach no harm whatever, under our law, to the mere drinking of whisky."

"Would you tell me then," I asked, "since you have not forbidden the making, nor the selling, nor the buying, nor the drinking of whisky, just what it is that you have prohibited? What is the difference between Montreal and Toronto?"

Mr. Narrowpath put down his glass on the "desk" in front

of him. He gazed at me with open-mouthed astonishment.

"Toronto?" he gasped. "Montreal and Toronto! The difference between Montreal and Toronto! My dear sir — Toronto — Toronto —"

I stood waiting for him to explain. But as I did so I seemed to become aware that a voice, not Mr. Narrowpath's but a voice close at my ear, was repeating "Toronto — Toronto — Toronto —"

I sat up with a start — still in my berth in the Pullman car — with the voice of the porter calling through the curtains "Toronto! Toronto!"

So! It had only been a dream. I pulled up the blind and looked out of the window and there was the good old city, with the bright sun sparkling on its church spires and on the bay spread out at its feet. It looked quite unchanged: just the same pleasant old place, as cheerful, as self-conceited, as kindly, as hospitable, as quarrelsome, as wholesome, as moral and as loyal and as disagreeable as it always was.

"Porter," I said, "is it true that there is prohibition here now?"

The porter shook his head.

"I ain't heard of it," he said.

❧XVIII❧

Merry Christmas

"MY DEAR Young Friend," said Father Time, as he laid his hand gently upon my shoulder, "you are entirely wrong."

I looked up over my shoulder from the table at which I was sitting and I saw him.

But I had known, or felt, for at least the last half-hour that he was standing somewhere near me.

You have had, I do not doubt, good reader, more than once that strange uncanny feeling that there is some one unseen standing beside you, in a darkened room, let us say, with a dying fire, when the night has grown late, and the October wind sounds low outside, and when, through the thin curtain that we call Reality, the Unseen World starts for a moment clear upon our dreaming sense.

You *have* had it? Yes, I know you have. Never mind telling me about it. Stop. I don't want to hear about that strange presentiment you had the night your Aunt Eliza broke her leg. Don't let's bother with *your* experience. I want to tell mine.

"You are quite mistaken, my dear young friend," repeated Father Time, "quite wrong."

"*Young* friend?" I said, my mind, as one's mind is apt to in such a case, running to an unimportant detail. "Why do you call me young?"

"Your pardon," he answered gently – he had a gentle way

with him, had Father Time. "The fault is in my failing eyes. I took you at first sight for something under a hundred."

"Under a hundred?" I expostulated. "Well, I should think so!"

"Your pardon again," said Time, "the fault is in my failing memory. I forgot. You seldom pass that nowadays, do you? Your life is very short of late."

I heard him breathe a wistful hollow sigh. Very ancient and dim he seemed as he stood beside me. But I did not turn to look upon him. I had no need to. I knew his form, in the inner and clearer sight of things, as well as every human being knows by innate instinct, the Unseen face and form of Father Time.

I could hear him murmuring beside me, "Short – short, your life is short"; till the sound of it seemed to mingle with the measured ticking of a clock somewhere in the silent house.

Then I remembered what he had said.

"How do you know that I am wrong?" I asked. "And how can you tell what I was thinking?"

"You said it out loud," answered Father Time. "But it wouldn't have mattered, anyway. You said that Christmas was all played out and done with."

"Yes," I admitted, "that's what I said."

"And what makes you think that?" he questioned, stooping, so it seemed to me, still further over my shoulder.

"Why," I answered, "the trouble is this. I've been sitting here for hours, sitting till goodness only knows how far into the night, trying to think out something to write for a Christmas story. And it won't go. It can't be done – not in these awful days."

"A Christmas Story?"

"Yes. You see, Father Time," I explained, glad with a foolish little vanity of my trade to be able to tell him something that I thought enlightening, "all the Christmas stuff – stories and jokes and pictures – is all done, you know, in October."

I thought it would have surprised him, but I was mistaken.

"Dear me," he said, "not till October! What a rush! How well I remember in Ancient Egypt – as I think you call it – seeing them getting out their Christmas things, all cut in hieroglyphics, always two or three years ahead."

149

"Two or three years!" I exclaimed.

"Pooh," said Time, "that was nothing. Why in Babylon they used to get their Christmas jokes ready -- all baked in clay – a whole Solar eclipse ahead of Christmas. They said, I think, that the public preferred them so."

"Egypt?" I said. "Babylon? But surely, Father Time, there was no Christmas in those days. I thought —"

"My dear boy," he interrupted gravely, "don't you know that there has always been Christmas?"

I was silent. Father Time had moved across the room and stood beside the fireplace, leaning on the mantelpiece. The little wreaths of smoke from the fading fire seemed to mingle with his shadowy outline.

"Well," he said presently, "what is it that is wrong with Christmas?"

"Why," I answered, "all the romance, the joy, the beauty of it has gone, crushed and killed by the greed of commerce and the horrors of war. I am not, as you thought I was, a hundred years old, but I can conjure up, as anybody can, a picture of Christmas in the good old days of a hundred years ago: the quaint old-fashioned houses, standing deep among the evergreens, with the light twinkling from the windows on the snow; the warmth and comfort within; the great fire roaring on the hearth; the merry guests grouped about its blaze and the little children with their eyes dancing in the Christmas fire-light, waiting for Father Christmas in his fine mummery of red and white and cotton wool to hand the presents from the yule-tide tree. I can see it," I added, "as if it were yesterday."

"It was but yesterday," said Father Time, and his voice seemed to soften with the memory of bygone years. "I remember it well."

"Ah," I continued, "that was Christmas indeed. Give me back such days as those, with the old good cheer, the old stage coaches and the gabled inns and the warm red wine, the snapdragon and the Christmas-tree, and I'll believe again in Christmas, yes, in Father Christmas himself."

"Believe in him?" said Time quietly. "You may well do that. He happens to be standing outside in the street at this moment."

"Outside?" I exclaimed. "Why don't he come in?"

"He's afraid to," said Father Time. "He's frightened and he daren't come in unless you ask him. May I call him in?"

I signified assent, and Father Time went to the window for a moment and beckoned into the darkened street. Then I heard footsteps, clumsy and hesitant they seemed, upon the stairs. And in a moment a figure stood framed in the doorway – the figure of Father Christmas. He stood shuffling his feet, a timid, apologetic look upon his face.

How changed he was!

I had known in my mind's eye, from childhood up, the face and form of Father Christmas as well as that of Old Time himself. Everybody knows, or once knew him – a jolly little rounded man, with a great muffler wound about him, a packet of toys upon his back and with such merry, twinkling eyes and rosy cheeks as are only given by the touch of the driving snow and the rude fun of the North Wind. Why, there was once a time, not yet so long ago, when the very sound of his sleigh-bells sent the blood running warm to the heart.

But now how changed.

All draggled with the mud and rain he stood, as if no house had sheltered him these three years past. His old red jersey was tattered in a dozen places, his muffler frayed and ravelled.

The bundle of toys that he dragged with him in a net seemed wet and worn till the cardboard boxes gaped asunder. There were boxes among them, I vow, that he must have been carrying these three past years.

But most of all I noted the change that had come over the face of Father Christmas. The old brave look of cheery confidence was gone. The smile that had beamed responsive to the laughing eyes of countless children around unnumbered Christmas-trees was there no more. And in the place of it there showed a look of timid apology, of apprehensiveness, as of one who has asked in vain the warmth and shelter of a human home – such a look as the harsh cruelty of this world has stamped upon the faces of its outcasts.

So stood Father Christmas shuffling upon the threshold, fumbling his poor tattered hat in his hand.

"Shall I come in?" he said, his eyes appealingly on Father Time.

"Come," said Time. He turned to speak to me, "Your room is dark. Turn up the lights. He's used to light, bright light and plenty of it. The dark has frightened him these three years past."

I turned up the lights and the bright glare revealed all the more cruelly the tattered figure before us.

Father Christmas advanced a timid step across the floor. Then he paused, as if in sudden fear.

"Is this floor mined?" he said.

"No, no," said Time soothingly. And to me he added in a murmured whisper, "He's afraid. He was blown up in a mine in No Man's Land between the trenches at Christmas-time in 1914. It broke his nerve."

"May I put my toys on that machine gun?" asked Father Christmas timidly. "It will help to keep them dry."

"It is not a machine gun," said Time gently. "See, it is only a pile of books upon the sofa." And to me he whispered, "They turned a machine gun on him in the streets of Warsaw. He thinks he sees them everywhere since then."

"It's all right, Father Christmas," I said, speaking as cheerily as I could, while I rose and stirred the fire into a blaze. "There are no machine guns here and there are no mines. This is but the house of a poor writer."

"Ah," said Father Christmas, lowering his tattered hat still further and attempting something of a humble bow, "a writer? Are you Hans Andersen, perhaps?"

"Not quite," I answered.

"But a great writer, I do not doubt," said the old man, with a humble courtesy that he had learned, it well may be, centuries ago in the yule-tide season of his northern home. "The world owes much to its great books. I carry some of the greatest with me always. I have them here —"

He began fumbling among the limp and tattered packages that he carried. "Look! *The House that Jack Built* – a marvellous, deep thing, sir – and this, *The Babes in the Wood*. Will you take it, sir? A poor present, but a present still – not so long ago I gave them in thousands every Christmas-time. None seem to want them now."

He looked appealingly towards Father Time, as the weak may look towards the strong, for help and guidance.

"None want them now," he repeated, and I could see the

tears start in his eyes. "Why is it so? Has the world forgotten its sympathy with the lost children wandering in the wood?"

"All the world," I heard Time murmur with a sigh, "is wandering in the wood." But out loud he spoke to Father Christmas in cheery admonition, "Tut, tut, good Christmas," he said, "you must cheer up. Here, sit in this chair the biggest one; so – beside the fire. Let us stir it to a blaze; more wood, that's better. And listen, good old Friend, to the wind outside – almost a Christmas wind, is it not? Merry and boisterous enough, for all the evil times it stirs among."

Old Christmas seated himself beside the fire, his hands outstretched towards the flames. Something of his old-time cheeriness seemed to flicker across his features as he warmed himself at the blaze.

"That's better," he murmured. "I was cold, sir, cold, chilled to the bone. Of old I never felt it so; no matter what the wind, the world seemed warm about me. Why is it not so now?"

"You see," said Time, speaking low in a whisper for my ear alone, "how sunk and broken he is? Will you not help?"

"Gladly," I answered, "if I can."

"All can," said Father Time, "every one of us."

Meantime Christmas had turned towards me a questioning eye, in which, however, there seemed to revive some little gleam of merriment.

"Have you, perhaps," he asked half timidly, "schnapps?"

"Schnapps?" I repeated.

"Ay, schnapps. A glass of it to drink your health might warm my heart again, I think."

"Ah," I said, "something to drink?"

"His one failing," whispered Time, "if it is one. Forgive it him. He was used to it for centuries. Give it him if you have it."

"I keep a little in the house," I said reluctantly perhaps, "in case of illness."

"Tut, tut," said Father Time, as something as near as could be to a smile passed over his shadowy face. "In case of illness! They used to say that in ancient Babylon. Here, let me pour it for him. Drink, Father Christmas, drink!"

Marvellous it was to see the old man smack his lips as he

153

drank his glass of liquor neat after the fashion of old Norway.

Marvellous, too, to see the way in which, with the warmth of the fire and the generous glow of the spirits, his face changed and brightened till the old-time cheerfulness beamed again upon it.

He looked about him, as it were, with a new and growing interest.

"A pleasant room," he said. "And what better, sir, than the wind without and a brave fire within!"

Then his eye fell upon the mantelpiece, where lay among the litter of books and pipes a little toy horse.

"Ah," said Father Christmas almost gayly, "children in the house!"

"One," I answered, "the sweetest boy in all the world."

"I'll be bound he is!" said Father Christmas and he broke now into a merry laugh that did one's heart good to hear. "They all are! Lord bless me! The number that I have seen, and each and every one – and quite right too – the sweetest child in all the world. And how old, do you say? Two and a half all but two months except a week? The very sweetest age of all, I'll bet you say, eh, what? They all do!"

And the old man broke again into such a jolly chuckling of laughter that his snow-white locks shook upon his head.

"But stop a bit," he added. "This horse is broken. Tut, tut, a hind leg nearly off. This won't do!"

He had the toy in his lap in a moment, mending it. It was wonderful to see, for all his age, how deft his fingers were.

"Time," he said, and it was amusing to note that his voice had assumed almost an authoritative tone, "reach me that piece of string. That's right. Here, hold your finger across the knot. There! Now, then, a bit of beeswax. What? No beeswax? Tut, tut, how ill-supplied your houses are to-day. How can you mend toys, sir, without beeswax? Still, it will stand up now."

I tried to murmur by best thanks.

But Father Christmas waved my gratitude aside.

"Nonsense," he said, "that's nothing. That's my life. Perhaps the little boy would like a book too. I have them here in the packet. Here, sir, *Jack and the Bean Stalk*, most profound thing. I read it to myself often still. How damp it is! Pray, sir, will you let me dry my books before your fire?"

"Only too willingly," I said. "How wet and torn they are!"

Father Christmas had risen from his chair and was fumbling among his tattered packages, taking from them his children's books, all limp and draggled from the rain and wind.

"All wet and torn!" he murmured, and his voice sank again into sadness. "I have carried them these three years past. Look! These were for little children in Belgium and in Serbia. Can I get them to them, think you?"

Time gently shook his head.

"But presently, perhaps," said Father Christmas, "if I dry and mend them. Look, some of them were inscribed already! This one, see you, was written 'With father's love.' Why has it never come to him? Is it rain or tears upon the page?"

He stood bowed over his little books, his hands trembling as he turned the pages. Then he looked up, the old fear upon his face again.

"That sound!" he said. "Listen! It is guns – I hear them."

"No, no," I said, "it is nothing. Only a car passing in the street below."

"Listen," he said. "Hear that again – voices crying!"

"No, no," I answered, "not voices, only the night wind among the trees."

"My children's voices!" he exclaimed. "I hear them everywhere – they come to me in every wind – and I see them as I wander in the night and storm – my children – torn and dying in the trenches – beaten into the ground – I hear them crying from the hospitals – each one to me, still as I knew him once, a little child. Time, Time," he cried, reaching out his arms in appeal, "give me back my children!"

"They do not die in vain," Time murmured gently.

But Christmas only moaned in answer:

"Give me back my children!"

Then he sank down upon his pile of books and toys, his head buried in his arms.

"You see," said Time, "his heart is breaking, and will you not help him if you can?"

"Only too gladly," I replied. "But what is there to do?"

"This," said Father Time, "listen."

He stood before me grave and solemn, a shadowy figure but half seen though he was close beside me. The fire-light had died down, and through the curtained windows there came already the first dim brightening of dawn.

"The world that once you knew," said Father Time, "seems broken and destroyed about you. You must not let them know – the children. The cruelty and the horror and the hate that racks the world to-day – keep it from them. Some day *he* will know" – here Time pointed to the prostrate form of Father Christmas – "that his children, that once were, have not died in vain : that from their sacrifice shall come a nobler, better world for all to live in, a world where countless happy children shall hold bright their memory for ever. But for the children of To-day, save and spare them all you can from the evil hate and horror of the war. Later they will know and understand. Not yet. Give them back their Merry Christmas and its kind thoughts, and its Christmas charity, till later on there shall be with it again Peace upon Earth Good Will towards Men."

His voice ceased. It seemed to vanish, as it were, in the sighing of the wind.

I looked up. Father Time and Christmas had vanished from the room. The fire was low and the day was breaking visibly outside.

"Let us begin," I murmured. "I will mend this broken horse."

THE AUTHOR

STEPHEN LEACOCK was born in 1869 at Swanmore in Hampshire, England. In 1876 the family emigrated to Canada and settled on a farm near Lake Simcoe. Educated at Upper Canada College and the University of Toronto, Stephen Leacock taught first at his old school of Upper Canada and later at McGill University in Montreal, where he rose to be head of the department of economics and political science. His first writings dealt with economics and Canadian history, but gradually as his true genius emerged he grew further and further away from this field and was attracted into his natural element of pure fun. Now he is remembered mainly as a humorist and the author of close to forty books of nonsense, including *Literary Lapses, Nonsense Novels, Sunshine Sketches of a Little Town, Behind the Beyond, Moonbeams From the Larger Lunacy, Frenzied Fiction, Short Circuits, Helements of Hickonomics, Our British Empire, Over the Footlights,* and *Arcadian Adventures with the Idle Rich.* At the time of his death in 1944, Leacock left four completed chapters of what was to have been his autobiography. These were published posthumously under the title *The Boy I Left Behind Me.* In 1946 it was decided by the Leacock Society to present a silver medal annually to the best book of humour published in Canada during the year. The Leacock Medal has become one of the outstanding awards in the literary world.

THE NEW CANADIAN LIBRARY

n 1. OVER PRAIRIE TRAILS / Frederick Philip Grove
n 2. SUCH IS MY BELOVED / Morley Callaghan
n 3. LITERARY LAPSES / Stephen Leacock
n 4. AS FOR ME AND MY HOUSE / Sinclair Ross
n 5. THE TIN FLUTE / Gabrielle Roy
n 6. THE CLOCKMAKER / Thomas Chandler Haliburton
n 7. THE LAST BARRIER AND OTHER STORIES / Charles G. D. Roberts
n 8. BAROMETER RISING / Hugh MacLennan
n 9. AT THE TIDE'S TURN AND OTHER STORIES / Thomas H. Raddall
n 10. ARCADIAN ADVENTURES WITH THE IDLE RICH / Stephen Leacock
n 11. HABITANT POEMS / William Henry Drummond
n 12. THIRTY ACRES / Ringuet
n 13. EARTH AND HIGH HEAVEN / Gwethalyn Graham
n 14. THE MAN FROM GLENGARRY / Ralph Connor
n 15. SUNSHINE SKETCHES OF A LITTLE TOWN / Stephen Leacock
n 16. THE STEPSURE LETTERS / Thomas McCulloch
n 17. MORE JOY IN HEAVEN / Morley Callaghan
n 18. WILD GEESE / Martha Ostenso
n 19. THE MASTER OF THE MILL / Frederick Philip Grove
n 20. THE IMPERIALIST / Sara Jeannette Duncan
n 21. DELIGHT / Mazo de la Roche
n 22. THE SECOND SCROLL / A. M. Klein
n 23. THE MOUNTAIN AND THE VALLEY / Ernest Buckler
n 24. THE RICH MAN / Henry Kreisel
n 25. WHERE NESTS THE WATER HEN / Gabrielle Roy
n 26. THE TOWN BELOW / Roger Lemelin
n 27. THE HISTORY OF EMILY MONTAGUE / Frances Brooke
n 28. MY DISCOVERY OF ENGLAND / Stephen Leacock
n 29. SWAMP ANGEL / Ethel Wilson
n 30. EACH MAN'S SON / Hugh MacLennan
n 31. ROUGHING IT IN THE BUSH / Susanna Moodie
n 32. WHITE NARCISSUS / Raymond Knister
n 33. THEY SHALL INHERIT THE EARTH / Morley Callaghan
n 34. TURVEY / Earle Birney
n 35. NONSENSE NOVELS / Stephen Leacock
n 36. GRAIN / R. J. C. Stead
n 37. LAST OF THE CURLEWS / Fred Bodsworth
n 38. THE NYMPH AND THE LAMP / Thomas H. Raddall
n 39. JUDITH HEARNE / Brian Moore
n 40. THE CASHIER / Gabrielle Roy
n 41. UNDER THE RIBS OF DEATH / John Marlyn
n 42. WOODSMEN OF THE WEST / M. Allerdale Grainger
n 43. MOONBEAMS FROM THE LARGER LUNACY / Stephen Leacock
n 44. SARAH BINKS / Paul Hiebert
n 45. SON OF A SMALLER HERO / Mordecai Richler
n 46. WINTER STUDIES AND SUMMER RAMBLES / Anna Jameson
n 47. REMEMBER ME / Edward Meade
n 48. FRENZIED FICTION / Stephen Leacock
n 49. FRUITS OF THE EARTH / Frederick Philip Grove
n 50. SETTLERS OF THE MARSH / Frederick Philip Grove
n 51. THE BACKWOODS OF CANADA / Catharine Parr Traill

n 52. MUSIC AT THE CLOSE / Edward McCourt
n 53. MY REMARKABLE UNCLE / Stephen Leacock
n 54. THE DOUBLE HOOK / Sheila Watson
n 55. TIGER DUNLOP'S UPPER CANADA / William Dunlop
n 56. STREET OF RICHES / Gabrielle Roy
n 57. SHORT CIRCUITS / Stephen Leacock
n 58. WACOUSTA / John Richardson
n 59. THE STONE ANGEL / Margaret Laurence
n 60. FURTHER FOOLISHNESS / Stephen Leacock
n 61. MARCHBANKS' ALMANACK / Robertson Davies
n 62. THE LAMP AT NOON AND OTHER STORIES / Sinclair Ross
n 63. THE HARBOUR MASTER / Theodore Goodridge Roberts
n 64. THE CANADIAN SETTLER'S GUIDE / Catharine Parr Traill
n 65. THE GOLDEN DOG / William Kirby
n 66. THE APPRENTICESHIP OF DUDDY KRAVITZ / Mordecai Richler
n 67. BEHIND THE BEYOND / Stephen Leacock
n 68. A STRANGE MANUSCRIPT FOUND IN A COPPER CYLINDER / James De Mille
n 69. LAST LEAVES / Stephen Leacock
n 70. THE TOMORROW-TAMER / Margaret Laurence
n 71. ODYSSEUS EVER RETURNING / George Woodcock
n 72. THE CURÉ OF ST. PHILIPPE / Francis William Grey
n 73. THE FAVOURITE GAME / Leonard Cohen
n 74. WINNOWED WISDOM / Stephen Leacock
n 75. THE SEATS OF THE MIGHTY / Gilbert Parker
n 76. A SEARCH FOR AMERICA / Frederick Philip Grove
n 77. THE BETRAYAL / Henry Kreisel
n 78. MAD SHADOWS / Marie-Claire Blais
n 79. THE INCOMPARABLE ATUK / Mordecai Richler

o 2. MASKS OF FICTION: CANADIAN CRITICS ON CANADIAN PROSE / edited by A. J. M. Smith
o 3. MASKS OF POETRY: CANADIAN CRITICS ON CANADIAN VERSE / edited by A. J. M. Smith

POETS OF CANADA:
o 1. vol. I: POETS OF THE CONFEDERATION / edited by Malcolm Ross
o 4. vol. III: POETRY OF MIDCENTURY / edited by Milton Wilson
o 5. vol. II: POETS BETWEEN THE WARS / edited by Milton Wilson
o 6. THE POEMS OF EARLE BIRNEY

CANADIAN WRITERS
w 1. MARSHALL MCLUHAN / Dennis Duffy
w 2. E. J. PRATT / Milton Wilson
w 3. MARGARET LAURENCE / Clara Thomas
w 4. FREDERICK PHILIP GROVE / Ronald Sutherland
w 5. LEONARD COHEN / Michael Ondaatje
w 6. MORDECAI RICHLER / George Woodcock
w 7. STEPHEN LEACOCK / Robertson Davies
w 8. HUGH MACLENNAN / Alec Lucas
w 9. EARLE BIRNEY / Richard Robillard
w 10. NORTHROP FRYE / Ronald Bates
w 11. MALCOLM LOWRY / William H. New
w 12. JAMES REANEY / Ross G. Woodman